HUSBAND, LOVER, HOLY MAN

○ ○ ○

Husband, Lover, Holy Man

An Intercultural Comedy

○ ○ ○

K. B. RAO

INTERCULTURAL PRESS

For information, contact:
Intercultural Press, Inc.
P.O. Box 700
Yarmouth, Maine 04096, USA

Book design by Jacques Chazaud
Cover design by Letter Space

Printed in the United States of America

97 96 95 94 93 92   2 3 4 5 6

Library of Congress Cataloging-in-Publication Data

Rao, Kanztur Bhaskara, 1926-
    Husband, lover, holy man: an intercultural comedy/K.B. Rao.
        p. cm.
    ISBN 0-933662-98-X
    1. Title
PS3568.A5955H8   1992
813'.54—dc20   92-9171
                                                            CIP

To SATYU and INDU
with affection.

PART ONE

○   ○   ○

HUSBAND

1

"Oh, Raj, she is beautiful, just beautiful," gushed Mrs. Neilson, look-ing at the snapshot. "And this is your son?" she asked.

"Yes. But that was when he was only three years old," Raj an-swered, looking over Mrs. Neilson's shoulder and brushing back his dark curls which had been gently disturbed by the bright plumage of her hat. "He is almost four and a half years old now," he added.

"Janice, come on over here," Mrs. Neilson called. "Look at this," she said, thrusting the snapshot at the tall, skinny woman who came forward, precariously balancing a paper plate heavily loaded with food from the buffet table in one hand and a cup of punch in the other. "Who is it?" Janice asked, peering through her butterfly-shaped, rhinestone and gilt-framed glasses, which gave her the appearance of a long-legged bird about to take off.

"It's Raj's wife," Mrs. Neilson beamed, proud that she had coaxed the snapshot out of Raj's worn-out wallet. "Isn't she adorable, just adorable," she exclaimed.

"My, my, you've been keeping it a secret, haven't you? Why, she's a doll," said Janice, who then turned around and called the others.

Soon there was a group of women of all shapes and sizes oohing and aahing over the attractiveness of the girl in the picture. Raj's face expanded with joy. Was his wife that beautiful? Of course, the snapshot had been touched up a little. But maybe she *was* really beautiful! He probably hadn't noticed it. But it must be true with so many ladies, and American ladies at that, praising her.

"You must tell us all about your wife. Everything," Mrs. Neilson said, getting up from her chair. Taking Raj's hand in one of her hands and the snapshot in the other, she led him to the front of the fireplace in the living room, where there were two chairs and a table.

"Girls, girls," Mrs. Neilson called out, tapping the table with a pencil. "If you've got your plates, please take your seats," she announced. The "girls," mostly in their forties, fifties, and sixties, all supposedly business and professional women, sat around the room balancing their plates on their knees. "Women, Thelma," someone muttered, in a tone of setting the record straight rather than debating the issue, "not girls." The other members of the group were obviously used to Thelma's incurable, old-fashioned style.

Raj sat in the chair behind the table, adjusted his tie, brushed back his hair, fingered the buttons on his jacket, coughed, and took a sip of water.

"Girls, we have a rare treat indeed tonight," commenced Mrs. Neilson, turning to Raj. "This is Raj. Of course, he has a long, long name which I cannot pronounce, so rather than make a fool of myself, I'm not even going to try." She laughed, and a few ladies tittered. Mrs. Neilson continued, "Raj is from India, and he's a graduate student at Avalon College. He's going to speak to us today. Of course he'd like to tell us about India, but I think he should first tell us about his own fascinating life. I've just seen a picture of his wife and she is just beautiful, simply adorable. I want Raj to tell us about her—I mean, how he met her, how he got married, and all about those ancient and wonderful customs they have over there. He's agreed to

4

answer any questions we might have. So girls, here's your chance. Just fire away after he's spoken." Mrs. Neilson laughed and sat down. Everyone applauded the best they could over the food teetering on their knees.

Raj nervously fingered the knot of his tie, took another sip of water, and stood up. This was going to be his eleventh speech in Avalon since he had arrived from India six months ago. He was the first Indian ever to come to this small Northern California town to attend Avalon College. He was their one and only foreign student. The college was proud of him, showing him off as its second biggest showpiece after the newly constructed Olympic-size swimming pool. Never had he been so eagerly courted by so many. He wrote long letters to all his friends back home in the South Indian town of Yalakki, describing in great detail his new fame and adulation. He lavishly exaggerated his achievements, such as his appearance on local TV, claiming that his speech on India's moral contribution to the world had been watched and listened to by millions of Americans.

Raj had come to enjoy both the spotlight and speech making. He had debated while at college in India; and, as a lecturer in English after he graduated, he had held forth on the glories of the English Romantic poets. So speaking was nothing new to him. The wide variety of Indian topics on which he soon became an authority in Avalon startled him at first, but he soon got used to it. He now spoke with the ease and confidence of a professional dilettante, switching from the caste system ("There is no caste in India. Not any more. It has been permanently abolished."), to nonviolence ("Indians are always peaceful all the time, except when they are provoked."), to language ("Everyone in India speaks some form of English."), to population control ("India is firmly against overpopulation, but wants to solve it in an amicable way."), to marriage customs ("More and more Indians are beginning to believe in love marriages.") which he used as a springboard to launch into a lengthy dissertation about his own love marriage.

"Actually, it was not a one hundred percent love marriage," he would say, as he was saying now after Mrs. Neilson had introduced him. "Half and half, you might say. A kind of synthesis between the old and new generation. For my parents' sake, I agreed to marry a girl

5

selected by them. For my sake, as the citizen of a new India, I selected the girl for love. So, obedience to parents, love for personal pleasure—a combination of the two. That is India's ability to synthesise, the noble contribution to India's cultural heritage." Now he was ready to take off—full steam ahead. When Raj got onto the cultural heritage track, there was no stopping him. He would lose himself in a torrent of words, purple rhetoric, Shakespearean quotations, and flights of fancy on the remote and distant past of Indian culture. This was his shining hour, to depart from the topic at hand and travel all over an India he had never seen, even waxing eloquent over the glories of the cave paintings and sculptures of Ajanta and Ellora (which he had first encountered in an art book in the Avalon College library).

But now, Mrs. Neilson interrupted him. He did not like that, but paused anyway. "Raj, I am sorry to interrupt you, but you must tell us all about how you met your wife. You simply must. She's just beautiful, really lovely," Mrs. Neilson gushed. Raj pardoned Mrs. Neilson when she praised his wife. He had begun to miss his wife, rather her cooking, and the thought evoked nostalgic memories of the rich and pungent aromas of the dishes she prepared. So he obeyed Mrs. Neilson. He might as well think aloud about his wife.

"My wife, if I may say so myself, *is* beautiful," Raj said, adjusting his tie with a smile. Mrs. Neilson smiled back and said "You certainly may!" The ladies who were not busy chewing potato salad or sliced ham joined in the laughter. Raj continued, "In more ways than one, my wife represents the perfect symbol of Indian womanhood, the very essence of which, so to speak, is obedience." Of course, she was not very obedient really, he reminded himself, for was there not a quarrel of some kind once a week between his mother and his wife? And didn't his mother open most of her conversations with him with the remark, "Your wife is disobedient to me again. You must talk to her." But then, why should he tell all these women? So, brushing back reality, Raj continued. "But my wife's obedience is harmoniously blended with a spirit of independence too—independence within herself, but obedience to a higher being. A quality of synthesis, which in a real sense is the essence of the Indian mystique." Raj sprinkled his lectures with words and phrases like "higher being," "Indian mystique," "eternity," "infinity," "immortality," and "immemorial," because he believed they gave to his talks an exotic, otherwordly spiritual resonance and satisfied the spiritual hunger from which Americans suffered, surrounded as they were by their gadget-cluttered culture.

Raj often thought of himself as a cultural and spiritual ambassador to America. In fact, that is how he had been described by his students and colleagues, and even by his own college principal in Bangalore when they had given him a farewell dinner wishing him bon voyage to America. "He goes today winging his way to America, as our unofficial cultural ambassador," the principal had said, "like another Vivekananda to take to the materialistic West the message of the spiritual East. It is not an easy responsibility. We wish him well," the principal had ended, garlanding Raj as he did so. Raj thrilled at these words, and since leaving India, he eagerly assumed this mantle of spiritual ambassadorship that had been thrust upon him.

"How did you meet her?" Mrs. Neilson questioned, interrupting him again and dragging him down to more basic matters.

"It was at a dance," Raj replied, letting loose his fertile imagination. "An Indian dance, I should add hastily," he said, "a dance where you observe dancers rather than dance yourself. In one way you dance too, as you respond to the rhythm of life, to that inner music of infinite beauty, to that divine music of the gods. Was it not John Keats, the British Romantic poet, who said 'Heard melodies are sweet, unheard are sweeter'?" Or was it Shelley who had said that, Raj wondered. Well, it made no difference to this audience anyway, he decided, and went on.

"Indian dance is very ancient. It is handed down from time immemorial from. . . ." But Raj's take-off point into the exotic features of the *bharatha-natyam* and the *kathakali* was rudely interrupted when a lady in the front row, trying to get up to fill her plate, was thrown off balance and knocked a glass of punch from her neighbor's hand. "I'm terribly sorry," she apologised, as other ladies helped to clean up. There was a minor commotion, but order was soon restored. Raj sipped some water, adjusted his tie, and started to hold forth on the art of Indian dancing. But Mrs. Neilson interrupted him again. "Were you both at the dance? You and your wife?"

A totally idiotic question, Raj thought; how could I have met her there otherwise? But controlling his irritation, he said, "Yes, we were both at the dance. We were both sitting in the front row, where most of the town's dignitaries were sitting," creating a scenario from his dream images. It was the way he had always wanted to meet a girl, a graceful girl with black lustrous hair, dark liquid eyes, and a supple body in a clinging silk sari with a delicate paisley border. They would meet in the Town Club. They would speak volumes with their eyes and ignite the bright flame of love. They would gently glide past each other, their very breaths caressing, communicating to each other their suppressed but smouldering passions. . . .

"And then what happened?" Mrs. Neilson questioned, awakening Raj from his fantasies.

"And then?" Raj repeated. "Oh, yes . . . and then we saw each other. And, if I may borrow an American expression, it was love at first sight," Raj said and laughed. "But you see, we could not talk with each other, or even openly smile at each other, for both of us coming from strict orthodox families—by that I mean well-to-do rather than religiously orthodox families—we had to maintain the code of conduct and moral decorum of our high, traditional society. But we knew mutually that we were attracted to each other. Our eyes flashed the message of our mutual desires. After all, the eyes are the windows of our souls. If you see, for example, some of the paintings and stone sculptures in Indian temples, you will see that the ladies there have the most expressive eyes. They have what one Indian poet described as liquid, limpid eyes. It is as though God were to have. . . ."

"You're not going to get away that easy, Raj. No diversionary tactics," Mrs. Neilson said, playfully pointing a finger at him.

"Ah, you want a full confession, Mrs. Neilson," Raj said smiling. "All right. You will get it. After the dance we did not see each other for quite a long time. I saw her go away in her chauffeur-driven car. But I made subtle enquiries and found out where she lived, who she was, and so on and so forth. She lived in a big bungalow, the biggest in Yalakki. After all, she is the only daughter of the town's richest man. Her father owned one of the biggest textile mills in South India. In fact, 60 to 70 percent of the cotton saris manufactured in the state of Karnataka, which is my home state, come from his mills."

One of the ladies in the second row got up. "I'm sorry, Thelma,"

8

she said to Mrs. Neilson. "I have to go. Jack's having some people over at the house from his convention. You tell me all about it later, will you? I'm sure I'm missing the best part. I am sorry," she explained and excused herself from the gathering.

That was the cue for a minor exodus as several other ladies followed her out, mumbling a variety of excuses.

"Raj, I think we were a little delayed in starting the meeting tonight. I know several of the girls have other things to attend to. So, if you don't mind, we'll go ahead with our business agenda. Any of the girls who want to leave after the business meeting can do so. Then we'll have the rest of the evening devoted to your talk. Is that OK with you?" Mrs. Neilson asked.

"Perfectly OK. Perfectly," Raj replied and sat down.

"We have to get a delegation together for the annual meeting in Bakersfield and I think Clara has a report on that," Mrs. Neilson started earnestly.

Raj drifted off as the ladies' meeting droned on. It would have been wonderful if indeed he had met his wife the way he had just described. Of course, it was not his wife but his secret sweetheart, Saroja, who had lived in the biggest bungalow in Yalakki. It was sweet, sensuous Saroja who used to attend dances at the Town Club, dressed in resplendent saris and rich jewelry. It was Saroja with her sumptuous breasts who went around Yalakki in her chauffeur-driven car. Raj had seen her from a distance, fantasised, hoped, and prayed that a miracle might happen to make him Saroja's husband and the son-in-law of Keshava Moorthy, Yalakki's richest man.

Raj had lost his heart to Saroja. "Ah, Saroja, sweet Saroja, you have stirred the very depths of my soul," he had confessed in one of his anonymous letters to her. In a two-hundred-page, unlined, card-board-bound notebook, which he had titled "Secret Whispers," Raj had written erotic poems and letters to Saroja. He had kept the notebook under lock and key in a battered steel trunk. Many a time he had thought of mailing the entire notebook to her with the inscription, "To Saroja, my secret sweetheart, from her secret lover." Instead, he had written her one eight-page, anonymous letter, which he had concluded by saying, "If you love me as I love you, please wear your rose-coloured sari on next Saturday evening when you go to the

Town Club. That will give me a reason for living." It was only after he had mailed the letter that he realised she would never know who the secret lover was. But that did not trouble him, for after all a secret lover had to remain secret. It was all part of the agony and ecstasy of true love. On Saturday he had watched the entrance to the Town Club from a distance, standing under the shade of the large mango tree. Saroja had never arrived that day, let alone in her rose-coloured sari.

If only he could have married Saroja, what a wedding that would have been, Raj thought, leaning back in his chair and abandoning himself to one of his dream journeys. The wedding would have been the talk of the town, with hundreds of important guests, including the chief minister of Karnataka, and maybe even a "wish-you-well-in-your-married-life" telegram from the president of India himself. Why not? After all, his would-have-been father-in-law had contacts in high political circles.

Such a wedding had taken place a few months later. But Saroja, the one and only daughter of Yalakki's richest man, had not even been aware of Raj's existence. On the day of her wedding, Raj had stood in the crowd and watched with envy and sadness the elaborate marriage procession make its way through Yalakki's main avenue, with a fourteen-piece band and fireworks. Saroja looked radiant and Raj felt his whole body ache with longing and desire. But then, Saroja had married Subramanya Swami, the rich son of another textile mill owner from Coimbatore. Money marrying money. Bank marrying bank. That is what the crowd had murmured as the procession passed by. That is as it should be, they had agreed.

Raj had been gloomy for a few days after Saroja's wedding. Wandering alone by the river near the abandoned Cobra Temple, life seemed empty; he had even contemplated suicide.

Then came Vimala, entangled in family ties. Events moved swiftly as pressure was put on him to marry her, to which he finally agreed. Remembering his wedding in the courtyard of the Kolar Primary School during the hot and humid month of June, that crowded courtyard where four other weddings were taking place the same day, Raj wondered now why he had decided to marry Vimala so quickly. Was it pressure from his mother? Was it desire to be a martyr? Was it the result of depression from the loss of Saroja, making him lonely and hungry for the warmth of a woman, any woman?

He shook his head, not wanting to brood on these questions. They left him melancholy. He sighed.

"Are you all right? Would you like a cup of coffee?" one of the ladies asked.

"Oh. . . ." Raj returned to reality. "No, no. I'm fine. Just thinking," he answered.

"We'll wrap up our business right away, Raj. And then we'll be ready to listen to your fascinating life. I can hardly wait," Mrs. Neilson said, leaning toward him and patting his hand.

"Take your time. Take your time," Raj said and took another sip of water.

After the wedding, Raj had tried in his imagination to will Vimala into becoming Saroja. But Vimala was not Saroja. Short and plump with just a high school education and six months in college (both in English medium), she did not come close to Saroja in grace or beauty.

Raj, who had fantasised a honeymoon in Kashmir with Saroja, settled for a mediocre hotel room in Bangalore. Here, with the sounds of heavy traffic outside the room, he performed his eagerly awaited duty as a husband. He had expected a lot, but Vimala had offered herself like a patient to a doctor, her eyes closed and her face turned away with an expression of controlled disgust. Even after he had switched off all the lights, Raj's intense imagination failed to evoke the image of Saroja and erase that of Vimala on that crucial night.

Later, as they lived in the house along with Raj's mother, his sisters and brothers, and their children, Raj continued his attempts to mould Vimala in the image of Saroja. But even to have an intimate conversation with Vimala proved difficult for him in the crowded house. There was no room he could call his own.

Raj took her out for an evening walk by the river to talk with her romantically. But Vimala's chatter was about more mundane matters, such as her differences with his mother and her sisters-in-law, about her need for another sari, and her desire to move away from the house and find a place on their own. Such seditious talk from one who was so silent at home disturbed him. He had tried to hold her hand, but she had moved away saying, "Not here in public. What will people think?"

Sex was something he took as that which belonged to him. Vimala offered her body as part of her duty. His exotic dreams of seeing her completely in the nude or behind a diaphanous sari remained unrealised. Their lovemaking took place late at night when he was certain that everyone had fallen asleep. He fumbled in the dark, as though searching for a light switch, and came quickly as a result of his pent-up desires.

Then she had become pregnant and returned in her sixth month to her mother's house—"for my first delivery"—coming back to Raj only after the baby was four months old.

"Now, Raj. We're terribly sorry that you had to sit through our little business session. But now we're ready," Mrs. Neilson said, re-awakening Raj from his reverie.

"Oh, yes," Raj stuttered, returning to the present.

"Ah, I see. You were a million miles away. Thinking of your wife, I suppose," Mrs. Neilson said teasingly.

"Well . . . in a sense, to be perfectly frank, yes," Raj said, getting up. There were only a few ladies left from the earlier large group.

"I don't think you need to stand up. We'll make it very informal. Just sit and talk. Take off your jacket if you want to. Make yourself comfortable. I'm sorry that the others had to leave. But this makes it much cozier and we can have a nice chat. Would you like some coffee?" Mrs. Neilson said.

"Yes, please have some," Mrs. Mary Gerber, the meeting's hostess, said. "I have a fresh pot brewing."

"Not now. I may have a cup later," Raj said.

"Any time. Just say the word," Mrs. Gerber said.

"I have really enjoyed attending this meeting," Raj commenced. "In fact I have learned many things. The way you ladies conduct the meeting so very efficiently is to be admired. In fact, I'm going to write about it to my wife. You see, she is the president of the Women's Club in my hometown, and she can greatly benefit from my description of your. . . ."

"Raj, is it a business and professional women's club, like ours?" Mrs. Neilson asked.

"No, not exactly. It is a club for women; most of the members are from the prominent families in the town. Mostly social meetings. Parties and cultural activities, with receptions for foreign guests and other visiting dignitaries. But very active. Very active," Raj fabricated.

"How exciting. Maybe our club and your wife's can have some kind of an exchange. Letters, gifts, and so on. I must bring this up at the next meeting," Mrs. Neilson said, making a note on one of her five-by-eight pink cards.

"Wonderful. You come up with great ideas, Thelma," said one of the ladies. The others mumbled their approval.

"That will be very good, the exchange project," Raj said. "It will bring greater understanding between America and India, which is as it should be. After all, are they not the world's two largest democracies?" he said rhetorically, and without waiting for an answer continued, "I will be more than willing to help you launch this exchange program. My wife can help too. Maybe there can be an exchange not only of letters and gifts but of members too. Of course, in the beginning one of the members can come here from there. That member can study your programs and go back. Ground can be prepared for one of your members to go over there. It will be excellent." Raj outlined his plan with excitement and enthusiasm.

"Maybe your wife ought to come as the first exchange member. After all . . ." Mrs. Neilson started.

"A very appropriate and brilliant suggestion, if I may say so, " Raj quickly interrupted, as though fearful that Mrs. Neilson might change her mind. "After all, my wife is the president of the club over there, and she already knows a little bit about your club through me. And I am going to write her a more detailed letter soon."

"And she *is* lovely. Just lovely," Mrs. Neilson said.

"Is her English as good as yours?" Mrs. Gerber asked.

"Definitely. She is a good talker. Very good," Raj replied, his mind racing fast and furiously. "She has no stage fright of any kind. She speaks boldly and clearly."

"This is most exciting. This project should be the highlight of our international committee. Let me go get the coffee. I think it's ready. Would you like a piece of apple pie with some ice cream?" Mrs. Gerber asked Raj.

"You must taste Claudia's apple pie. It's yummy! Just out of this world," Mrs. Neilson urged.

"If you say so and describe it with such mouth-watering phrases, how can I refuse?" Raj said and laughed.

Over coffee and pie a la mode, the small but enthusiastic group discussed plans for bringing Raj's wife as an exchange visitor to Avalon. They agreed to press the other members to support their proposal, set up fund-raising and welcoming committees, and get busy making arrangements.

"By the way, what's your wife's name, Raj?" Mrs. Neilson asked.

"Saroja . . . no, I mean Vimala," Raj said, correcting himself.

"Just lovely, lovely," Mrs. Neilson said and poured another cup of coffee for Raj.

That night as he lay in bed, Raj thought how good it would be to have his wife and son come over. Here in Avalon, away from his crowded kith-and-kin-infested house in Yalakki, he could ultimately realise his dream of moulding Vimala in the image of Saroja. With all these pills, powders, creams, pastes, vitamins, and protein-crammed foods so persistently advertised on television, maybe he could work a miracle on his wife. She would emerge like the graceful Saroja, probably better than Saroja. He would then have his own, his very own, fair lady. She could mingle with these active American women, improve her style of speaking English, learn how to drive a car . . . such endless possibilities. The best part would be that with the coming of his wife, he would have her cooking. He could stop eating in the college cafeteria, save money that way. He could move into an apartment. Mrs. Neilson had promised her help in finding a furnished place. He could get away from dormitory living. Ah, such sweet prospects crowded his mind.

Of course, his coming to America itself was a miracle. How could a poor lecturer like him ever have come to America, particularly with all the labyrinthine rules and regulations that the government of India had set up to prevent people from going abroad. Raj felt glad as he looked back on how it had come about.

An American student, Steve Preston, had delivered a lecture about life in American universities at Raj's college. Raj attended that lecture and listened with rapt attention as Preston talked about

American campus life and about the many students from India who worked part-time at a variety of jobs to earn money for their continuing education. Preston mentioned one Indian student in particular, an enterprising individual who had started a small Indian snack shop close to a college campus in New York and gradually expanded it to a full-scale Indian restaurant employing several Indian students as waiters. The waiters were making good pay and even better tips. "There's American capitalism at work," Preston had proudly declared.

Immensely impressed, Raj met Preston after the lecture and volunteered to act as his guide in Yalakki. He escorted Preston to the Mahalakshmi Temple, so that the young American could take photographs of the holy man there, who was meditating in a state of *samadhi*. He had a long bushy beard and was in such deep meditation that he was totally unaware that birds had built nests in it. "Fascinating, just fascinating," Preston repeated and snapped away with his telephoto-lens-equipped Nikon. When Preston indicated a curiosity about Indian family life, Raj had taken him to his house, where Preston kept bumping his head against the low ceiling but managed to say *namaskara* with folded hands to each and every member of the crowded household.

At the end of the day, while having a glass of buttermilk in Bhatta's Neo-Café, Yalakki's famous restaurant, Preston thanked Raj for his time and help. It was then that Raj confided to Preston his secret desire to go to the United States to study. Preston suggested that he might take a chance by writing to Avalon College. "That's my alma mater. I got my bachelor's degree there a long, long time ago. It's a small college, but they might be interested in having a foreign student. Give it a try. They do offer a master's in English. Tell them you heard about the college from me. I know the president, Dr. James Rose. He was my history professor when I was there. I'll drop him a note, too, about you. No guarantee that it'll work, but try," Preston had encouraged.

Raj wrote and Avalon College responded favorably by granting him a tuition-free scholarship and free room and board in the dormitory, along with a fellowship in the English Department, which would give him some money for his incidental expenses. In the euphoria of going to America to study, Raj was not concerned that he could only get another master's in English, even though he already had one from the University of Mysore in India. The administrators at Avalon College were happy that someone from as far away as India had heard of their college. Besides, they wanted a genuine foreign student from a *real* foreign country, not someone like Douglas Spencer, who, although he came from Canada, looked and talked very much like an American.

Raj managed to secure a loan from the bank to meet his transportation costs, took study leave from the college, and ultimately arrived in Avalon.

Now, Raj dreamed of holding cultural evenings for his American friends at his house as soon as his wife and son arrived. His wife would prepare a variety of dishes, and after a leisurely meal, the cultural part of the evening would commence. He would persuade his wife to sing a song or two, and he would teach her a few hand movements from the *bharathanatyam*. As she entertained them, telling in this way stories from Indian myth, Raj would interrupt and interpret.

These cultural evenings at his house would truly make him the unofficial cultural ambassador of his country. Raj wished his wife could come the very next day. Thinking of all that was about to happen, he felt homesick for the first time since his arrival in Avalon.

2

Mrs. Neilson had succeeded in persuading a close friend of hers, an elderly widow whose ancestors had at one time served as missionaries to India, to provide a rent-free, furnished house for Raj and his family.

Four months later, after Mrs. Neilson's valiant fund-raising, many potluck dinners, hundreds of phone calls, innumerable committee meetings, and the appointment of further committees to be in charge of their Indian guest, Raj's wife arrived with their son, Kittu, at the San Francisco International Airport.

Raj and twelve members of the welcoming committee, including three husbands who had been drafted into driving three carloads of them, were on hand to greet Vimala and Kittu.

As Vimala and the boy emerged from customs, Raj realised with a shock that his wife was not the lovely person he had been imagining her to be. She was exactly the way she had been when he had last seen her—plain, simple, and homely. Her hair was in disarray, her eyes weary, and her posture sloppy as she struggled along with their son, a heavy airflight bag constantly slipping from her sagging shoulder. Kittu looked weary, a bit pugnacious. He clung to his mother rather than rushing forward to embrace his father, in spite of Raj's repeated instructions in several long, detailed letters to his wife. "When you arrive, there will be many people to greet you. You must smile and say 'Hello, darling,' to me. Do not be shy. Be modern and up to date. You must smile all the time. I repeat this instruction. Smile. Teach Kittu to say, 'Hello, Daddy.' Teach him to smile and tell him to come forward and hug me. This is very important because the first impression must be very impressive," he had written.

As soon as Vimala came within earshot, she started speaking in Kannada about her long, frightening plane journey, with people all around her eating all that red meat and making her stomach queasy. "First thing I must do is take a hot bath, very hot, and then wash off with a very, very cold bath to cleanse myself," she said, contorting her face in disgust. Raj attempted to cover his embarrassment by introducing her to the members of the welcoming committee. "We are delighted to have you," Mrs. Neilson said, offering her a bunch of flowers. The others murmured their delight. In trying to make up her mind whether to shake Mrs. Neilson's hand or greet her in the traditional Indian style, Vimala got confused. The bunch of flowers fell to the ground. As Raj stooped to pick them up, Vimala offered a limp, banana handshake to Mrs. Neilson.

She started to speak in Kannada again to Raj, "Kittu wants to go to the bathroom, immediately." Raj tried to take him, but Kittu refused to budge from his mother, even after a gentle coaxing by Mrs. Neilson, who offered him a large box of beautifully wrapped candy. "You give it to him, Raj," Mrs. Neilson said. "He's shy, isn't he? My, he is cute, and those large brown eyes. Lovely, just lovely," she added. Kittu grabbed the box of candy from his father. Raj felt like spanking his son right then and there.

"You also come," Raj instructed his wife and, excusing himself from the welcoming group, hastened with his family toward the rest rooms.

After they had walked a distance, Raj let loose angrily at his wife. "You have put me to shame. Is that the way you behave? Why are you wearing that drab sari? Did you read my letters? Did I not write long, detailed, minutely descriptive letters with specific numbered instructions on what to do, what to say, how to behave, and so on and so forth? I told you to wear the rose-coloured sari with the bright red border when you got off the plane. Did I not write you a short speech saying, 'I am delighted to be in America. Thank you for all your help.' Why did you not say those words when you were introduced? Why? Look at your hair! It is like a big bird's nest. You look like you have just got out of bed. Why can't you speak English? And what happened to him?" Raj said looking at his son, who had squatted on the ground and was trying to untie the ribbon that held the box of candy. "What is wrong with him? He thinks I am a devil or something. Why didn't you teach him to say, 'Hello, Daddy. I had a wonderful plane trip' just like I asked you to? Do you know how much trouble these ladies have gone through to get you here? And you . . ." he stopped, for his wife had burst into tears.

"Stop crying. You have already brought enough shame on me," Raj said.

She continued, muffling her sobs with the end of her sari, while Kittu's attempts to open the candy box had turned the yellow and green ribbon into a Gordian knot.

"You are just like your mother," Vimala said, between her sniffling and her sobbing, "always abusing me. I thought I would get away from her, and now as soon as I arrive, just like her, you attack me. Did I want to come? You have not even asked me how I feel. No food, no sleep. I was so frightened. It is my fate. My karma. Just my karma to be abused by someone or other all the time. I am not like my young sister. She is lucky. Her husband treats her like a queen. Me? I am a slave. My fate!"

People began to stare at them. Raj wished that the earth would open up and swallow them. A young sailor passing through the lobby even tried to take a picture of their domestic squabble with his Instamatic. Raj was aghast, but his sense of dismay and shock increased when he noticed that his son had abandoned the unknotting of the ribbon and had started to unbutton his shorts.

"Not here!" Raj screamed in spite of himself, and hastily dragged his son to the rest room.

By the time he returned, Mrs. Neilson had picked up the box of candy and was comforting Vimala.

"Oh, Raj, your wife is exhausted," Mrs. Neilson said, drawing Vimala close to her. When Raj attempted to explain, Mrs. Neilson interrupted him. "Oh, we understand. This long trip, the jet lag, and everything else. All so strange and different to her. I'll drive you back to Avalon. All of you sit in the backseat, relax, and talk things over. And do it in your own language, too. I won't mind a bit, not one bit." She smiled and gently stroked Vimala's hair.

"That will be very nice, Mrs. Neilson. Thank you. But what about your plans to spend the weekend in San Francisco with your friends?" Raj asked.

"Don't give it another thought. I'll do it another time. The important thing is to get you folks to Avalon and get you settled in your home," Mrs. Neilson replied as she reached out to stroke Kittu's cheek.

3

The others in the welcoming party headed toward San Francisco. Mrs. Neilson drove Raj's family to Avalon. It was nice and cool, and they stopped at a drive-in for some breakfast. Out of respect for Vimala, Mrs. Neilson refrained from ordering eggs and had pancakes instead, and so did Raj. He decided to break it gently to his wife, later, that he had made a minor departure from his pure vegetarianism since arriving in America by eating eggs.

They all felt much better after breakfast, and the three of them sat back in the large, spacious station wagon.

"Are you comfortable there?" Mrs. Neilson asked. "If it's too windy, tell me. I can close the window."

"We are very happy. Thank you for your kindness," Vimala replied, carefully articulating the words.

"You are quite welcome, my dear," Mrs. Neilson replied.

Raj wished that his wife had spoken more casually, not with such studied precision, as though repeating a memorised sentence. Anyway, at least she had spoken in English and said something nice, he reflected and counted his blessings.

"Do you feel better now?" Raj asked his wife in Kannada. "Mrs. Neilson, I hope you don't mind our talking in. . . ."

"Not one bit, Raj. Go right ahead and don't mind me at all," Mrs. Neilson replied.

"Thank you very much," Raj said.

"I was only able to bring lemon pickles for you," Vimala said.

"That's all right. How is everybody at home?" Raj asked.

"Actually, I prepared mango pickles. From first-class mangoes, perfect for pickles. My brother himself specially brought them from the market. But you know how it is!" she said with a sigh. "I should not say it, but still I must tell you, give you the complete picture. If not you will think that for some strange reason I did not bring you mango pickles, your favorite pickles."

"That is fine. Lemon pickles will do," Raj said.

"I made two big jars. Big jars. What happened? Your sister took them. Both jars. Both of them. What can I say? If I said one word, one small word, your mother would oppose me right and left. After all, your mother has to support your sister. Why? Because your sister is your mother's daughter. Who am I? Just a daughter-in-law! So I kept my mouth shut. So I asked my brother to bring home some lemons. But this is not the season for pickle-making lemons. So they are still sourly bitter, the pickles I made. What to do? If I had insisted on the mango pickles, at least one jar, there would have been a war. And as you know I am by nature a very peaceful person. I never like fights. I get terrible headaches after every fight. So. . . ."

"Lemon pickles are just fine. Tell me about home affairs. Is everyone all right?" Raj asked.

"Yes, yes, everyone is all right. Do you know what your mother said? She said I was taking you away from her. Why should I do that? She said that I wanted you to go to America. Why not? I said. After all, I want my husband to study and advance and bring honor to our country. Then she started to accuse me by saying that I *forced* you to go to America so you would send for me. Did I force you? I did not. Why should I want to come to America? Who cares for America? In fact, two weeks from now, my third and youngest brother, Seenu, is getting married into a very rich family. Why not? He is a medical doctor. Of course he still has three or four years to actually become a medical doctor. But he has applied for admission. My brother has influence and somehow, one way or other, he will get admission. Once you get admission, you are definitely going to become a doctor. Doctors make lots of money as you very well know. Seenu wanted me to stay. 'Akka, do not go. Stay for my wedding,' he pleaded. But I still sacrificed the wedding and came. Why? Because you asked me to come. We must send my brother a wedding gift from America. Is it very expensive to send them a refrigerator? After all, if we send a gift, it must be impressive. We must keep up our status. Of course, I must not say this, but only in the interest of truth, let me say it. Do you know what your own very favorite sister said when she heard that I was thinking of sending a refrigerator to my brother? She said, 'Raj cannot afford it.' Do you know in front of whom she said it? She said it in front of that loudspeaker-voiced Nagappa family. And everyone in that family is already tom-tomming, propagandising, that you are bankrupt and barefoot in America. That is what your favorite sister does to you. Publicly she tells everyone that you are poor. She is jealous of you. That is the truth, take it or leave it. Everyone, including your mother as well. But do you know what I have been telling everyone in Yalakki? I told everyone, 'Look, my husband is very intelligent. He draws thousands of rupees in salary in America. When he gives lectures, hundreds and thousands of Americans listen to him in pindrop silence.' You remember that lecture you gave on television? Well, I showed everyone that letter you wrote describing how you gave that lecture. I was very proud that all these Americans belonging to such an advanced country are admiring you. I am proud of you. But your mother and sister, oh, no, they do not want me to be proud of you. 'Do not go to America. You will ruin him,' they kept saying. Would you have invited me if I am going to ruin you? I felt like weeping at that remark. I wept all night. Do you have a television set? Will you be on it? I am so eager to see it." She poured out her words in a continuous torrent.

"But you see about the refrigerator . . ." Raj started.

"Even a secondhand one will be all right. What is that?" she asked, looking out of the window.

"Supermarket. A shopping center. But you see, even a second-hand. . . ."

"Oh. Poor Kittu, he has fallen asleep," she said.

They moved close to each other, making room for Kittu to stretch out.

"You must remember that life in America is very expensive," Raj said.

"Same in India, too. Very bad. Double, triple price for every-thing. Evening price higher than morning price. Rationing also some-times. Rice is full of stones and sand. You buy one kilo, half of that is full of stones. Then water difficulty. No water at all some days. They allow water at two in the morning for two hours till four. Then shut off. Not even a drop. Who had to fill up the water tank? Who else but me. Your sister, mother, other kith and kin are enjoying sleep. So I get up at two, fill the tank, go to sleep for two hours, get up again. You think this two-hour sleep I had was peaceful? Oh, no. A lot of noise from neighbours. Gundappa family, always fighting, always argu-ing. Then after the fight they start to wash clothes. It was hell. No peace and quiet at all. I am tired from working. Do you have servants? I hope I can get some rest from work in America. How many servants do we have?"

"There are no servants in America. Only very very wealthy peo-ple have one or two. Machines do all the work. You see, even a secondhand refrigerator . . ." Raj started, eager to root out his wife's plans to send a gift to her brother.

"Have you seen Vasu?" she interrupted.

"Which Vasu?" Raj asked, irritated at the way she was jumping from topic to topic.

"Vasu. Don't you know Vasu? He is in America. The son of Mutthappa on Keshava Moorthy Road. Husband of Malu, daughter of retired subdivision officer of Banavoor. He has left her. That is definite," she pronounced judgment.

"Who has left who?"

"Vasu has left his wife, Malu. I know it. But still Vasu's mother came to our house, tears in her eyes, requesting me to find out the truth. Is it true Vasu has married an American wife? Have you seen?"

"Seen who? What? Where?" Raj asked with mounting anger.

"The American wife of Vasu."

"All rumours. Besides . . . never mind," Raj was shaking his head.

"Poor Malu, leaving her like that. Vasu has no shame, no responsibility. I must find out the truth and write to Vasu's mother. Somehow I must get a picture of Vasu's American wife. I have Vasu's address. His mother gave it to me. I will show you," she said, and started digging into her airflight bag and pulled out a worn diary, flipped through the pages, and pointed to an entry with her finger.

"Dr. E. M. N. Vasudevan, 118 Elm Street, Bridgeport, Connecticut," Raj read. "Oh, that Vasu!" he remembered.

"Ah, you remember him? Is he close by? Can we go in front of his house and . . .?"

"Connecticut is about three thousand miles away. Besides . . ."

"I must somehow find out. He is nothing but a loafer and wife deserter."

"You must not say such things without knowing the facts."

"Why not? Truth is truth. Do you know what happened to your sister's husband? Not Shuba, your older sister Champa. Very shameful. He is suspended. Took bribes. Do you remember what I told you one night two years ago? 'How can Champa buy new silk saris every month?' Makes money, yes. But how? Under the table. Takes bribes left and right from contractors. But he was found out by anticorruption committee. They are corrupt too. I know, that is the truth. Anyway your sister's husband's job went pfut! But your mother is covering up and telling everyone 'My son-in-law is not well, therefore he is on leave!' Leave, huh, permanent leave. I know. My brother has high contacts in anticorruption committee. So he found out. He told me. Shameful of Champa's husband. No dignity at all. Now the other matter is. . . ." She continued, unabated, untiring, jumping from one subject to another, full of gossip.

Raj wondered whether he had made a dreadful mistake in bringing his wife to America. Finally worn out from her chatter, she said, "I'm very tired. No sleep. Too much talk. I still have much to tell you. But we can talk about it later," and leaning back, went to sleep.

"She's quite a talker, isn't she?" Mrs. Neilson said.

"Yes. Filling me in on family matters," Raj replied.

They reached Avalon late in the afternoon.

4

The following few days proved trying for Raj, answering his wife's innumerable questions. He looked back with nostalgia to those days in India when, because of the lack of privacy, he did not have to converse with her.

He took her to the supermarket, but one glimpse of the meat counter with all the bloody cuts of beef, chicken, and lamb packed and displayed so openly sent her right outside again, with the end of her sari lifted to cover her mouth. At home she kept washing the vegetables and fruits over and over again, giving them a quality of guilt by association for having been in the same place, under the same roof, as meat. She read the tin cans carefully, including cartons of salt and bags of sugar, to make sure that no meat had been sneaked in surreptitiously. "You cannot trust these nonvegetarians," she declared. "They are always trying to convert you like missionaries." Raj was driven to the end of his patience repeatedly assuring her that there was no meat in salt and sugar. He also gave up the idea of confiding to her about his liking for eggs and abandoned his earlier plans of building her up with vitamins. He realised that she had enough strength already.

Kittu sat glued to the TV with a fresh box of candy. Raj tried to take away the candy, but his wife protested vehemently. "Poor boy. Let him eat. There are no good chocolates in India these days. You remember you sent one box one time? Kittu did not get any at all. Your brother's son swallowed the entire thing," she said, putting a candy into Kittu's mouth very affectionately and caressing his cheeks. She popped one into her own mouth as well. "Next time bring those chocolates where there is fruit in the center," she instructed Raj.

Vimala, however, proved a solid hit with the Women's Club. Her naiveté, her unembarrassed questions, her bubbling curiosity in wanting to examine everything from a pepper grinder to an electric hair dryer, her constant, ebullient overflow of language with juicy gossip and comments about Indian life whetted the appetites of the women she came into contact with. They liked her heavy, unadulterated "foreignness" in their midst. Besides, Vimala had a unique, no-holds-barred approach to life, a quality that proved often to be infectious.

Raj, on the other hand, was constantly embarrassed, especially the time when she visited a bathroom in one of the ladies' homes and came back ecstatic about its perfumed, antiseptic cleanliness. She went on praising it and started comparing it with the typical Indian bathroom by saying, "You see in India, there is a large opening in the. . . ." Raj had to literally shout in Kannada, asking her to shut up. She did, but not before saying, "You see, the Indian wife is a slave. She must obey her husband." Why are there men in attendance at a meeting of this women's club?

Vimala wrote home long, detailed letters in Kannada, to her brother and innumerable friends, describing her life in America. She exaggerated the affluent life that she and her husband and son were leading in Avalon. "We have two cars. Two television sets," she wrote, and listed all the various electrical household gadgets she had seen in other people's homes, including some that she herself created, like the machine which obeyed "all your directions as you lay on the bed and shouted out your instructions. I am teaching this machine how to prepare Indian food." She increased Raj's fellowship amount to a few more figures. When Raj objected to her telling such lies, she retorted by saying, "You must not belittle yourself. You must keep up your status." She also slyly hinted that Raj, too, took liberties with the truth, like how about that one where he was supposed to have been on TV and listened to by thousands of people?

She began to get more letters from her friends and relatives than Raj did. They praised her, envied her good fortune in being in America, and listed many items they wanted her to bring back for them. She patiently recorded these requests in a notebook. There were several requests from her various relatives urging her to use *her* influence on her husband to use *his* influence on Americans to get *their* sons scholarships so they could study in America. She dutifully urged Raj to help these aspiring young men, and when he replied that it was impossible to do so, she bitterly accused him of being selfish.

But her special project was to send a refrigerator to her newly married brother. All conversations either began with this request or converged on it. Raj began to dread coming home. But her superb cooking was the bait. In this she constantly excelled. She cooked every kind of Indian dish with gourmet delight, so that Raj eagerly looked forward to dining in spite of the inevitable talk about the refrigerator.

Raj could smell the curry and the rich sauces even before he entered the house. She had abandoned all the formalities of sitting at a table American style. Raj wore his dhoti, and all three sat comfortably on a carpet they had flung on the kitchen floor and dug uninhibitedly into their hills of rice and tanks of thick vegetable curry, surrounded by a variety of other side dishes. Hardly able to get up after such a hearty meal, all three then sat on comfortable lounge chairs in the living room with tall glasses of iced water and, in a land-of-lotus-eaters' lethargic state induced by the hot, heavy, spicy food, watched TV.

Raj found it very difficult to study or work on his term papers after the evening meal. Now that his wife and son were here, his expenses had increased, and he had taken a part-time job in the college library. Thus, what time was not taken up in attending classes and managing the departmental assignments he received was spent working in the library, including evenings and weekends—at least that is what he told himself. Daily his resolutions to get down to work—later or after dinner or early in the morning when he was fresh—fell apart. His grades dropped, and he began to worry when one of his professors suggested he give up his library job and pay more attention to his academic work.

Raj needed the library job, for Vimala was getting into the spirit of American life. She had obtained a credit card in a department store and was buying presents for her friends. Raj realized with a shock that his monthly fellowship stipend, his part-time wages, and the allowance that his wife got from Mrs. Neilson's group disappeared long before the next payments were due.

Raj put his foot down when he found out that she had been

making installment payments on a large refrigerator to send to her brother. Things erupted in the house that night. Raj told her that henceforth he would not come home for dinner, that he would study instead, and that she ought to stop preparing a feast each and every night. Then he picked up her plastic credit card and bent it back and forth over and over again until it broke and told her that he'd call the store and cancel the hold she had put on the refrigerator. "Your brother will not get that gift," he declared.

Raj resolutely stuck to his plan even though in the mornings now, Vimala would talk to Kittu loudly for Raj's ear: "Kittu, what shall we have for dinner this evening?" And Kittu would list a menu which Vimala knew would make Raj's mouth water.

On the fifth evening of his peanut-butter-sandwich and back-to-study resolution, Raj was in the library. Around nine he needed a break and walked down to the graduate lounge. He got himself a cup of coffee from the vending machine and decided to smoke, a habit he had kept secret from his wife. Lynda, a tall, skinny, redheaded classmate of his, joined him on the couch. They started to discuss Robert Frost, about whom a term paper was due.

A few minutes later Vimala appeared in the lounge and unceremoniously started to attack him in Kannada. "Your one and only son is about to die and you sit here like a maharaja, smoking, drinking, enjoying life with an American girl."

Raj, flustered and embarrassed, put out the cigarette, mumbled excuses to Lynda, and ushered his wife out of the lounge.

Kittu was sick, a severe case of stomachache. The doctor, who was hastily summoned, suggested that the boy cut down on his starchy food and sweets. "Give him fruits and salads. See that he exercises. And if I were you, I'd ration his TV viewing as well. I'm afraid he won't be able to go to school for a few days," the doctor said.

"Going to school no problem," Vimala said. "He is not attending any in first place."

"Not going to school?" the doctor asked.

"My husband cannot afford it," Vimala said.

Raj was furious. "Not exactly . . ." he tried to explain.

"I don't want to interfere in your family affairs, but we've all got to have an education. Good-bye," said the doctor and left.

27

"Why do you always speak without thinking? You were the one who said that Kittu must not go to public school because you needed his company. If you stopped buying all those gifts and that refrigerator, we'd have some money to send him to private school," Raj accused her.

"Always it is me. Always it is the refrigerator. What about your spending money on cigarettes? What about your spending money on that American girl?"

"Which American girl?" Raj interrupted.

Vimala continued without answering him. "Now I know why you do not want to eat at home. You probably enjoy eating meat with that American girl."

"Which American girl?" Raj screamed.

"How many do you have?" Vimala retorted.

Raj hoped that Vimala was not aware of his fascination and flirtation with Virginia Gleason, a fellow graduate student whose interest in Indian philosophy had brought them together.

"How many?" Vimala demanded vigourously.

"I talk in the library with Lynda, who's in my class and you make a big. . . ."

"Who cares how many you have," Vimala dismissed with indifference her earlier curiosity and began again to bemoan her fate, her karma. "Why should I blame that loafer Vasu? At least he did not openly parade in the library with his American paramour for his wife to see. You bring me all the way from India, refuse to eat my food, and then flirt with this Lynda. Tell me the date you are going to abandon us so that. . . ."

"Shut up, just shut up," Raj shouted.

"Why shut up? Because I am telling the truth? Don't give me any money to buy a refrigerator. I will buy one with my own money." It was a challenge.

"Your own money?"

"Yes."

"From where?"

"From where? From my hard work."

"What hard work?"

"Why should I tell you? You show no interest in my work. For two months I have been asking you to type one short letter for me. Have you done it? No, you have not."

"What letter?"

"A letter to appear on that 'make a million' TV show."

"That is stupid. You will never make a million."

"How do you know? Answer me. Do you think you can appear in a movie?"

"What movie?"

"You think I don't know? I know all about those letters you are writing to Hollywood, saying that you are an actor, that you can act like that English actor Peter Sellers, that you even look like him, a little bit. If my wanting to make a million is stupid. . . ."

So, she had gone through his papers and seen the draft of a letter he had planned to send to several directors in Hollywood.

Raj did not allow her to complete the sentence. He slapped her. Kittu started crying. Vimala stared at Raj, then burst into tears and flopped on the sofa.

Raj rubbed his palms in anguish and recrimination. He had not meant to slap her. He felt ashamed that he had lost control. He wanted to go over to her, embrace her, say he was sorry. But instead he looked around the house and continued his tirade. "See how shabbily you keep this house. Clothes all over the place. Smell of food, papers, all over. Disgusting, just disgusting. You have ruined me. Do you know that? Just ruined me. I am a fool to have asked you to come. Just a fool. Stop crying. What will the neighbours think? Stop it."

She continued to sob and mumbled something.

"What did you say?" Raj roared.

"Cursing my fate. I should have stayed home, listened to my brother Seenu, and attended his wedding. Now, here I am, in a strange country with a sick son, angry husband, and on top of that . . ." her voice faded.

"On top of that what?"

She remained silent.

"What on top of that?" Raj insisted.

She dried her tears and stood up. "I am pregnant. Yes, that is what is on top of that," she said firmly.

"Oh, God."

"Why blame God?"

"How long have you known?"

"A month, two, what does it matter?"

"Why didn't you tell me. Why?"

She stared at him, wiped her eyes with the end of her sari. Then facing him squarely she said, "Tell you? When? When you don't come home for food, when to tell you?"

"Stop talking, please. Go to sleep, go on," Raj said and walked out of the house slamming the door.

An hour later he called Mrs. Neilson from the college library and said, "Mrs. Neilson, sorry to disturb you. But I need your help." She asked him to come over right away.

Three weeks later, Mrs. Neilson drove Raj, Vimala, and Kittu to the San Francisco International Airport.

"Finish your work and return safely," Vimala said to Raj before boarding the plane. "I shall not tell anyone about your troubles. I will keep up your status. Bring all the things I have listed. But you must bring the car, Chevrolet, like my elder brother has said. We can sell it and make a good profit. My brother has good connections in the black market community. We need the money to keep our status in town. Is there any other family in all of Yalakki where husband, wife, and son have all been to America? I will tell my younger brother Seenu that because of postal delays and shipyard strikes and so on, there is a bit of a delay in his getting the gift of the refrigerator. I will definitely make mango pickles and send them by airmail," Vimala kept chattering.

"All right, all right. You must go now. There is not much time left," Raj attempted to stop her lengthy speech.

Raj stroked his son's hair and pinched his fat cheek playfully. Then he took out a big bar of chocolate from his pocket and gave it to him.

Kittu smiled as he took the chocolate. Vimala nudged her son. "Go on, say what I told you to say," she said.

"Thank you . . . Daddy," Kittu said hesitantly in English and quickly clung to his mother's sari.

"See, how he has learned all the American customs," Vimala

beamed proudly. "Just like me, he also has become Americanised. Is that not so, Mrs. Neilson?" she asked.

"Yes, dear, yes, of course," Mrs. Neilson said, hugging Vimala.

"Mrs. Neilson, you simply must come to India. You must. Then you can come to Yalakki. In some small simple way, I must return your kindness," Vimala said.

"I'd like that, Vimala, I'd like that very much. You never can tell. I might just do that one of these days. Just hop on a plane and give you a surprise visit," Mrs. Neilson said.

"Not surprise visit, Mrs. Neilson. Definitely, no. No, do not surprise us like that! Do not shock us that way. We must have some time to prepare a warm welcome for you, in our own simple humble way. Not grand welcome, but full of affection," Vimala said.

Mrs. Neilson laughed. "You are sweet, dear. Take care. Have a safe trip home. And do write to me when you get some time. I'd love to hear from you."

Vimala nodded. She looked at Raj and added, quickly, her lips trembling, "Darling," feeling embarrassed for having thus addressed her husband.

"Just becoming Americanised to please my husband," Vimala said by way of explanation to Mrs. Neilson. Tears formed in her eyes.

Mrs. Neilson hugged her back with a smile and murmured, "I understand, my dear."

Vimala wiped her eyes with the edge of her sari and briskly walked into the boarding area leading Kittu by the hand.

PART TWO

○   ○   ○

LOVER

1

Dear Virginia:

(As you can see, I still prefer to address you as Virginia, rather than as Ginny. Virginia is purer.)

You must forgive me for this inordinately long delay in replying to your thoughtful, kind, sympathetic (even romantic, if I may be permitted to use that adjective) letters.

I received all three of them.

I relied on the fact that since you had not carried out the threat you had indicated (let me quote your exact words from your letter, "If I do not get a prompt reply to this, my second letter, I shall not write you again"), you would continue not to do so.

I assumed that the above threat would be repeated in the third letter, and also in the fourth letter, and so on. But alas, to my dismay, the fourth letter has not arrived for quite some time—three and a half months, to be more or less exact.

So, I believe (I reluctantly conclude) that this time you have indeed carried out your threat by cutting off your correspondence (eagerly awaited, as always) with me.

I plead guilty to the charge.

I am to blame for not taking you seriously. I do not imply by this statement that I take you lightly. I do take you seriously, but I had not taken your either-this-or-else ultimatum seriously because you are one of those few people who leaves the door open slightly. You never shut it completely.

Please keep the door open, Virginia, please!

I therefore write this letter with a compelling sense of urgency mingled with profound heartfelt apologies.

Even as I write these words I am hounded by the fear that you might Air-India yourself instead of airmailing another letter (my letter and you, crossing each other like birds at night) and journey down to see me. This gnawing fear of your impulsive arrival in order to shock me with an unexpected surprise (surprises are unexpected, I fully realise) visit has begun to haunt me with such passionate intensity that I've been unable to sleep for the past two nights.

Last night your feared surprise arrival did indeed become a reality. In my dream, I mean. Rather I should say, in my nightmare. Therefore, I decided to write you without further procrastination.

Let me explain last night's dream, alias nightmare.

I am sitting in a room. In my house. I am not involved in doing anything in particular. I have the local newspaper in my hand, but I am not reading it.

Enter, my wife. She is in a very excited state. She is flashing danger signals. Her hands gesture violently, her red bangles jingle and sparkle like sparks of fire (to match her angry eyes) as they catch the light from the naked bulb dangling from the ceiling.

She says (with her built-in megawatt stereophonic voice), in her usual exclamation-punctuated style of speaking: "Why are you sitting here doing absolutely nothing when one of your friends is facing grave problems trying to find someone's house? Get up. Go out. Help her. Hurry up."

That reference to "her" makes me break out into sweat, for in a lightning flash upon my inward eye, your image appears. I exclaim to

36

myself: "Oh my God, Virginia's here! At my very doorstep or close to it."

But with remarkable outward calm I ask my wife: "Which friend? Where? What problem?"

My wife (who is always long-winded) surprises me by her answer-to-the-point response: "The problem of finding the correct house. On this street. Some American lady."

Again, I calmly reply: "How do you know it is an American lady? Further, that person you refer to need not necessarily be my friend. Further, what guarantee is there that I am in a position to guide her, for I may not know that someone's house she is looking for. Everyone on this street may know me, but I may not know everyone who knows me."

Even as I utter these words, my mind is working fast and furious to devise ways and means of getting out of my house and thus avoid greeting you, if in case it should be you. Even as I plot this escape, I hear the faint but nervous voice within me saying: "It is Virginia. She is here." But there is one consoling thought that creeps up. Virginia will have difficulty in finding my house. It will take time. So I have some time at my disposal.

And you may ask, why will you have difficulty in finding my house—dream or no dream?

When the houses of my two brothers went up, my first brother's house was assigned number 10½. According to all canons of town planning, logic, and urbanology (is there such a word?), my second brother's house should have been given the number 11½. But there's the rub! As my logic teacher in college used to say: "If there were no ifs and buts India would be a great country." But there are ifs and buts and so on and so forth. By the time my second brother made up his mind (he's the slowest member in the family; he was born delayed, in the tenth month, which may partially explain his habit of postponing all his actions even after he has made decisions) to construct a house in the open space in front of my first brother's house, one of the neighbours on the right-hand side of our property built a house in the open space in front of his own house.

This is another thing I have noticed since my return. Open spaces are no longer open, for small houses are coming up all over.

Therefore, this new house built by our neighbour was assigned 11$\frac{1}{2}$ which (the number eleven and a half, not the house) rightfully belonged to my second brother. Thus my second brother became 12$\frac{1}{2}$ instead of 11$\frac{1}{2}$.

To summarize: My house, number 9$\frac{1}{2}$, is *behind* 12$\frac{1}{2}$ and 10$\frac{1}{2}$.

After my return to India I became quite upset. My sense of logic and order which I had picked up in America during my two years and five months there was outraged at this haphazard system of assigning numbers to houses.

I know that I told you several times, when I was in Avalon, that if ever you did come to my little town, you would have no difficulty in finding my dwelling place.

My house is a large bungalow, with two tall coconut trees on either side of the entrance. On the white wall in black letters is boldly inscribed the number 9$\frac{1}{2}$. That is the way I have already described my house to you. But as I just mentioned, my second brother, who inherited a part of the property, built a house on his share, which happened to be directly in front of my house. Therefore, you would have difficulty finding my house now.

According to my wife, my two brothers were not really interested in putting up their houses so as to relegate my house (although slightly larger than their two houses) to the back, to darkness, to a sort of limbo, but they were actually influenced and coerced by their respective wives (with whom my wife does not see eye to eye; one of my sisters-in-law is cross-eyed anyway) into doing so.

My brothers are not living in their respective houses. They work in other towns and have rented out their houses. These houses (let me explain here that when I say houses I do not want you to get any great and glorious idea of houses such as you are accustomed to in America) are a mere four walls (sometimes only three because the fourth wall of one house becomes also the fourth wall of another) with some covering or roof over them (zinc sheets or asbestos sheets).

Actually (to be blunt), they are not houses at all but small cubicles. There are a total of four families staying in these two houses, with a total population of somewhere in the neighbourhood of twenty or twenty-two. Some of the older members, particularly the men, do not sleep at night in their respective cubbyholes because the cubbyholes, being cubbyholes, cannot accommodate all of them. So they walk over to the Shiva Temple, which is in the center of the town, and sleep in the courtyard.

I have also noticed (without any special efforts of observation on my part) that three women among these four families are pregnant. So it is safe to say, and correct to assume, that there will be some additions to the existing population of these four families within the not-too-distant future. The presence of these pregnant women is also one of the reasons (since they take up more space as a result of the extra burden they are carrying) why the menfolk have to sleep in the courtyard of the Shiva Temple at night. And I am certain that even after the children are born—the burdens unloaded and the stomachs receded—the menfolk must continue to sleep in the Shiva Temple. I suppose that is poetic justice in one way for, after all, they (the men, that is) are responsible for imposing these burdens carried about by their spindly legged, emaciated wives. Of course, the men may sleep better in the courtyard of the Shiva Temple without constantly being awakened by the restless crying of the babies.

The very first evening of my arrival in my hometown, in front of my house which I could not see, I declared boldly with controlled anger: "We are not mere numbers. We are individual people. The City Corporation which gives these numbers to residences must show some human consideration for the people living in these houses." Everyone who had gathered to meet me, to welcome me, murmured their assent. A distant uncle (actually not too distant) of mine who was in the gathering went a step further and said, "Hear, hear" and applauded. Applause, somewhat undernourished, followed.

A few words about my somewhat-distant-yet-not-that-distant uncle. Pardon the digression, Virginia, but I must give you the complete picture.

My uncle used to be a high school mathematics teacher. Now retired, he still has a reputation in this town for his strong discipline. People bemoan the fact that present-day teachers in India are not strong disciplinarians and look back with nostalgia to the days when people like my uncle held up the principles of high scholarship. My uncle had a nickname when he was a teacher, which was "Ear Twister," for he had a propensity for twisting the left ear (always the left because of his left-handedness) of students whenever they made the slightest mistake in addition, subtraction, division, multiplication, or any such mathematical calculations.

After leading the applause, he made a speech supporting my advocacy of the human dimension in urban planning: "One of my former students by the name of Shree Pada is presently working in the City Corporation Offices as a humble clerk. My American-educated and American-returned nephew Raja Ram Pattabhiramanna, M.A. of world-famous California university, must write a letter to the Corporation's Commissioner requesting that house numbers be assigned chronologically instead of haphazardly. Somewhat simultaneously, give or take a day or two this way or that way, I will put in a word to my former student, namely Shree Pada, clerk in the Corporation Offices. In deference to me as his former teacher, he will bring my nephew's letter to the attention and action of the Commissioner. Never underestimate the power of a poor clerk. He has the power to make letters appear and disappear. Careful cultivation of my clerks can bring proper rewards swiftly," my uncle concluded.

Others applauded. My uncle beamed because he had stolen the show, and he continued: "You will be doing a great service to our entire town and to all of India if you take a lead in this matter and bring order where there is chaos, and system where there is no system, and numerical logic where there is haphazardness. I have a total distaste in coming to your house. It is highly embarrassing to me to tell my friends that my American-returned nephew's house is $9^{1}/_{2}$ behind $12^{1}/_{2}$."

At this point my wife interjected a proposal that I should write the above suggested letter on my typewriter that I had brought from America. My uncle supported her by saying: "Definitely. It will get more response if the letter is composed on the American typewriter where the letters will stand out bold, strong, fat, and well-fed, not weak and undernourished like the letters from Indian typewriters."

I said to my uncle with a touch of humour, "I hope you have not twisted the ear of this former student of yours who is now a clerk in the Commissioner's Office." My uncle missed my humour (which is natural, being a mathematician he is very cut and dried; of course Lewis Carroll is an exception!) and said very gruffly: "What if I did

40

twist his ear. It was for his own good. Has he now not got a secure job? Even now when he sees me, he thanks me for having twisted his ear as a result of which he has not made one small, slight, minuscule error in addition or subtraction since."

I did type a letter on my Smith-Corona portable (made in Canada, bought in London on my way from America) addressed to the Corporation's Commissioner, asking that residence numbers be assigned chronologically and not haphazardly.

There was no response. When I pressed my uncle about what his former student was doing about it, my uncle dismissed the whole thing with another of his aphoristic statements: "Former teachers are quickly forgotten by their former students."

I pursued the matter with a few more letters to the Corporation, and the Corporation Officers started giving me explanations, verbally, as to why assigning house residence numbers haphazardly was not a threat to individuality but rather a mark of rugged individuality. For example, "Why should $9^1/_2$ be before or even after $10^1/_2$? Why not $9^1/_2$ after $12^1/_2$? Why? After all, India does not want to imitate the Western world with its capital located in Washington, D.C. India wants to do things Indian-style, haphazardly, if necessary."

By then I had lost my enthusiasm and reverted to my Indianness with that self-consoling feeling that maybe the haphazard numbering of the houses in our compound had a deep significance, the meaning of which would make itself known later, that it might have been divinely ordained, if you want to use such an expression.

Now at this moment (in the midhalf of my nightmare) when I realized that you could have arrived, I realized the significance of this deeper, divine, ordained meaning. If indeed you had come, and if indeed you were looking for my house, bearing number $9^1/_2$, then you were bound to have difficulty in locating it, thereby giving me time to leave the house and not be there by the time you found it.

As a matter of fact, some of the letters I get are often addressed:
Raja Ram Pattabhiramanna
No. $9^1/_2$
(which is behind House No. $12^1/_2$ and
House No. $11^1/_2$ in the same compound)

The postman, of course, is used to such elaborate addresses. The most elaborate address I can think of is that which belongs to an acquaintance of mine living in Delhi. It is as follows:

A. B. Ahuja
Upstairs Corner House No. 39/22
Plot 4, Block 8, New Layout Section 11B-32/41C
Very Close to New Women's College
Mahatma Gandhi Road (new)
Delhi, India

Sometimes Indian addresses are little miniature letters themselves. So much for Indian postal addresses.

To return to the nightmare. My wife continues to harangue me: "I am positive," she says. "I am cent percent certain she is an American woman. Even though I didn't spend as long as you did in America, I can easily say without one little bit of difficulty who is an American woman and who is not. Go and help her. After all, were not Americans always asking us, May I help you, when we were there? Get up. Put on your suit and tie and quickly go out."

I ask: "A suit and tie just to tell that American woman about someone's house?"

She replies: "Why don't you put on American blue jeans? You have always said that you had no occasion to wear them. Now is the time. The moment she sees you in blue jeans, she will feel relieved that she is able to find someone with whom she can talk."

I reply: "Neither suit nor blue jeans. Leave me alone."

My wife is not silenced. "I think you must wear blue jeans. After all, were not Americans sometimes wearing saris or lighting sandalwood sticks and saying to us, This will remove your homesickness? I think your wearing blue jeans will in some way remove this American woman's homesickness."

Virginia, have you met my wife? Of course you have. Remember that time you met her very briefly and you said: "She's a shrew!" I asked: "Did you say my wife was shrewd?" And you, out of politeness, said: "Yes." Later you told me you had said shrew and not shrewd. I

42

complimented you on your ability to sum up a person's character just like that, so quickly. My wife is a shrew. Very definitely! She's become more of a shrew, if that's possible.

She continues her nonstop breathless chatter, ceaselessly, endlessly, meaninglessly, waving her hands, pointing her finger. I get up, not to wear blue jeans and help this lost American woman (who very well may be you) but just to get the hell out of my house. By now I am positive that it is you, and that you are coming closer and closer to my house, and that you even run into the postman and ask him for directions, and that he gives them to you. You are at my doorstep! You knock! Knock! Knock!

I shout, scream, or some such hysterical thing. Then I awakened, sweating. My son was crying. He always is. And my wife was asking what was the matter and why had I screamed as though I was falling out of a plane. My mother rushed into the room from the kitchen asking what was wrong.

My wife immediately said: "It is a bad dream and, if it has occurred so early in the morning, then it means that the dream will become a reality. We must visit the Temple and offer proper worship. Maybe a complete milk bath to Lord Ganesha to overcome whatever obstacles there are. Have I not been persuading you to visit the Temple with all my breath ever since your arrival? My throat has gone dry by telling you to do that. But you do not pay attention to anything I say. Who am I that you should listen to? Just your wife, that is all. After you returned, the astrologer said to me with utmost respect, 'Vimalamma, I am telling you in the interests of both of you that a purification ceremony is necessary for your husband. Absolutely necessary. Just a simple one will be enough. I see certain planetary positions that are not in the best interests of your husband's progress. There are some formidable obstacles. With proper *pooja* and offerings to a couple of priests, these fiery obstacles can be converted to smoke and made to disappear with the wind. Certain spirits have to be satisfied. I will do it,' he told me. Did I not tell you what he told me? And did not your mother who never agrees with me on anything agree with me on this? Tell me, did I not tell you this or did I not tell you this?"

"Yes, yes, you told me. Let us not discuss the matter anymore," I said wearily.

43

"It has to be discussed," she said. "Why not? Further, you should not have arrived on a Tuesday."

I said: "What has Tuesday got to do with it? The correct superstition is that arriving from a journey on a Tuesday is all right as long as you do not start your journey on a Tuesday."

She started again, tying the end of her sari around her waist, in a challenging, come-on-let's-wrestle style: "But, you see. . . ."

I just walked away toward the back of the house to go to the lavatory. It was occupied. Three people were waiting in line. They were the tenants from the houses in front. Somehow, accidentally (my wife says deliberately), both my brothers and their respective architects (that is much too grand a term to describe those who built these crooked walls and leaking roofs) had forgotten to provide the tenants of their respective houses with lavatories. So they have been using the one lavatory at the back of my house (belonging rightfully to us for our use—me, my wife, my mother, and my son) at first on a temporary basis, but like everything else in India, the temporary has become permanent. Of course, whenever anyone from my house (those mentioned above) has to answer nature's call (as the expression is used to describe in India what in America is often more directly referred to with one of your vivid Anglo-Saxon four-letter words), those tenants who are about to use the lavatory make way for us. We have first priority.

My wife has often used this priority. She goes to the lavatory and sits there for an unduly long period, causing great anxiety among the women from the front houses. The men mumble, grumble, and give up and go away in search of facilities in some other place. Maybe to the high school which is not too far from where we live (providing they are not obstructed by the High School Servant), some other person's house, or even ingeniously improvise some facility (and don't ask me how with your bubbling American curiosity).

Unfortunately, the women are stuck, anxious and impatient, waiting for my wife to hurry up her business. And when she comes out only to find that I have called her out to make place for one of the ladies, her fury is . . . furious (for want of a better word).

Her argument is that her sit-in demonstration in the lavatory will make the women complain to their husbands, who in turn will complain to my brothers and thereby pressure them for the establishment of additional facilities.

I have explained to my wife that this will never happen. If the tenants complain to my brothers, they will reply by asking them to leave if they are not satisfied. Since house accommodations are so scarce, these tenants will not leave. They will grumble and mumble, have little fights and long arguments, compel themselves to be patient, find other facilities on a temporary basis, and continue their temporary existence which like everything else in India will become permanent (sorry to repeat myself) as long as they live.

I have chastised my wife for her sit-down pressure tactics in the lavatory but it is of no use. To put it bluntly, I have an incorrigible wife. Frankly, I do not have much energy left to fight her. This shrew cannot be tamed. Between her haranguings and the extreme heat, I feel drained of all my energies. If Mrs. Neilson had not come to my aid in Avalon, I would not have been able to pack her off to India by myself.

Virginia, I will continue this letter tomorrow or later today. I will mail this off now so that it will be on its way to you.

I am in one way finding some relief by sharing my problems with such an understanding person as you.

With all my best, yours,

Raj

P.S. Do not reply to this letter until you get my complete letter.

2

Dear Virginia:

After posting the earlier letter a few days ago, I forget the exact date, I became doubtful about whether I had made myself clear or not.

So, to make myself perfectly clear (to quote one of your former presidents) I am writing this letter immediately.

Please do not Air-India yourself, or for that matter, Air-any-other-airlines yourself to India until we discuss the matter.

Another letter will follow.

Yours,

Raj

P.S. To be even more clear and to the point: DO NOT COME!!!

3

Dear Virginia:

I hope you have received my two earlier letters, one long, one short.

It is quite possible that you may get this letter simultaneously or even earlier than the one long and one short letters. (After you have dropped the letters in the mouth of the postbox, you have no control over how fast or slow they reach their destinations.) If that should happen, please read the letters in their proper sequence.

Also I just realized that I might have (know I have) forgotten to write the date on the two earlier letters, plus other formalities to be observed in letter writing, such as addresses at the top and so on. You must forgive me. I have been under great pressure. To be frank, this letter-writing-to-you business is in many ways physical torture for me. I have not yet organized myself in my room. I do not as yet have a table, a chair, etc., etc., in order to position myself properly to write. There are many reasons for this disorganized state of affairs. I shall not go into all that now.

All I want you to do when you read these letters, sitting in your pleasant yard among the flowers and enjoying that aroma of California tranquility, is to visualize me sitting in a room (why mince words? in my cubbyhole) on a worn-out coil mattress and using the uneven surface of a bedroll as my table, plus the anxiety hanging over my head like the sword of Damocles concerning my wife's constant but unannounced entrances and exits (alas too few exits!) into my cubbyhole, plus her repetitive nose-butting-in question: "What are you writing all the time?" In fact, she was here five minutes ago, even as I was writing this letter. She had come to take her sari, and as it would happen the sari was on the worn-out mattress upon which I was sitting. You can very well guess the rest. The interruption was even more severe in that I had to get up, crumple this letter (the reason for the unironed look of the paper), and allow her to take her sari. She came close to the truth when she said: "What are you writing all the time? Do you have a secret sweetheart in America?" Fortunately at that time, my son started hollering for his mother. (He is taking after her more and more, Virginia. I have not noticed one good trait he's taken from me. He is his mother's son, definitely.) If you can visualize all this, then you will understand the haphazard tone and style of these letters.

Without unduly indulging in purple-prose rhetoric, I can say that these letters are sincere documents from my naked heart.

One more truth. Let me say it before it slips away. I miss you. Very, very much. For the first time (and maybe for the last time) my wife uttered truth when she said that I was probably writing these letters to a secret sweetheart in America.

I will unashamedly declare it in this letter. Yes, you are my secret sweetheart, Virginia. If I have embarrassed you, I am sorry. Ignore this statement, censor it, feel no compulsion to respond to it.

In this case let love be on one side. I will talk no more about love. I promise. Only if you refer to it in your reply will I resurrect my secret love for you from the deep subterranean recesses of my heart. If not, let it stay deeply buried there.

But the fact that I miss you, with or without the connotations of romantic love, is, however, a fact.

As a matter of fact, on the fourth day after my arrival (ah, I remember the Christmas party singing you did: "On the fourth day of Christmas my true love gave to me") I began to miss you desperately and started to write you a letter to give you a sort of private report on the state of body, mind, and spirit pertaining to one American-returned Indian human being (namely me).

But I did not complete the letter/report. (I am a good starter but poor completer. An inability to maintain and sustain initial enthusiasm is my weakness, my Achilles heel, so to speak.)

As a matter of fact, the incomplete letter referred to above had a further disaster. It was lost, rather, misplaced. But after careful search among my papers (such a grandiose term: "My Papers") consisting of free travel folders, picture postcards, airline maps, paper nap-kins, and such other totally useless items I had picked up only to impress my relatives about my travels, I found the above referred to incomplete letter.

I would have attached this letter as Exhibit A just to demonstrate to you that while I have been negligent in answering your letters, I had already started writing you a letter even before I received your first one, but it is now too dog-eared. We don't have any dogs or cats in our house. My mother would never tolerate them. On this matter she is prepared to take a stand and fight with my wife. Of course, such an encounter will not take place because my wife equals my mother in her passionate hatred of animals. Of course there are two animals they do not hate, but rather respect them: the cow and the snake.

Anyway, to get on with this letter, let me briefly summarise from my incomplete, lost but found, considerably dog-eared letter. In this letter I had said (after addressing you as Dear Virginia): "Just a note to let you know that I arrived in India three days ago. Did you get my postcards from London and Frankfurt?" Although I had written in my London postcard, "Enjoyed my stay in swinging London," to be perfectly honest I did not enjoy my stay in London. In fact, my stay in London was most miserable. The immigration people at Heathrow Airport, where my Pam Am flight arrived, seemed very reluctant to admit me inside London. They thought I was one of those stateless Asians who wanted to settle down in London. I had to assure them over and over again that I was merely passing through and had no intention of settling down in Britain.

"Why are you visiting London?" "What is your purpose?" These two basic questions were asked over and over in different ways with different words. My answer: "I am passing through. I want to visit the theater. I want to go to Oxford and Cambridge. I want to go to Stratford-upon-Avon."

They scrutinised my Indian passport as though it was a subversive document, held a miniconference among themselves, looked me over with their X-ray eyes, and then reluctantly let me enter their country whose most glorious period of history was made possible by India, the Jewel in the Crown.

The British immigration officials were also giving a rough time to a Black from America. He looked just like James Baldwin. Of course, I had never seen James Baldwin face-to-face, only a picture of him on one of the book jackets. And, as a matter of fact, I read in the next day's paper that it was James Baldwin, and that he had been so disgusted with the treatment he received that he had flown back to Paris.

I should have done that too, flown back to some other city or directly back to India. But I didn't. My life seems to be, at least up to this point, a matter of I should have done so and so or such and such a thing. When will I start "doing"? If I do start, I do not complete. I guess like most Indians, my life is noun-centered rather than verb-centered.

Anyway, I enjoyed Frankfurt and wish I had spent the money and time I spent in London in Frankfurt. The Germans are very friendly and pleasant. Maybe if there were fewer Indians in London, the British might have liked me too. But there are too many Indians. That's the truth. If we are to be liked we should make ourselves scarce (like diamonds or gold). That is why population control makes sense, any way you look at it.

I will not have any more children. My wife wants two more. One boy, one girl. She has put in an order. I have said no. In this case I want to be a bad beginner (or not beginner; not even take the first step) because you cannot start a baby and then stop, except through abortion, in which act I do not believe. On this, my wife and I see eye to eye. (By the way, in case I have not told you, my wife lost that baby which she was carrying when she left the U.S.) Serious doubts about my decision to return to India began to crowd in my mind like nasty cockroaches. First of all, I had not obtained a degree, the primary purpose for which I had made this overseas trip to America. Of course, I knew that even if I had accomplished my purpose and secured a degree (or sheepskin as you Americans term it, though I have never seen one made from the skin of sheep, which makes me wonder if your football, which you often call a pigskin, is really made from the skin of a pig, which in some ways is a better thing to do with a dead pig than eat it) there was no guarantee that it would in any manner, shape, or form improve my prospects for advancement professionally, so to speak. Further, I could not see myself being of indispensable use

49

to my country even with my degree in American Literature, with specialization in the poetry of Robert Frost. Further, it would have been totally ridiculous and utterly useless to teach Robert Frost to my miserable students (sitting thigh to thigh on long wooden benches, in the small stuffy room close to the railroad, so that each time the goods train went by I had to pause in my appreciation of Robert Frost) who had never seen snow, and probably never would.

Enough of Robert Frost. I've wasted enough time on a subject for which I have no use. (Actually speaking, I did not have any use even in the first place. I only agreed to do my thesis on Frost because that so-called faculty advisor of mine, Michael Carr, guided me toward such a decision.) It was only later I found out that Carr had a selfish purpose in mind. He was writing a book about Frost (may his book be never completed, never, never published. And never read if my first two wishes don't come true!) and was therefore using me and Tom Slear (you remember him? The big, blond, bearded boy with the sad Jesus face?) to do his research for him. I am to blame because, as Tom Slear put it so appropriately, we should have researched Carr's motive before embarking on the research of Frost. (All that is now so much snow over the roof.)

That's enough digression. Back to the homeward flight.

Everything looked very gloomy. The dark ink-black clouds outside my plane window only added to my gothic mood of apprehensive melancholy. The thought that minute by minute I was being taken closer and closer to that dreaded meeting with my talkative wife and my sullen and ill-mannered son further darkened my suicidal mood.

To plunge or not to plunge out of the plane window, that thought too crossed my mind. But it was an actionless thought. As you can see, I am writing this letter.

Further, no one, not even my wife, knew that I had lost my old job at the college in my hometown. I had extended my term of study leave by three more months without the authorised permission of my college principal, so he had mercilessly sacked me. The truth is, the principal looked upon me as a threat to his own position, because he knew that an American-master's-degree holder specializing in the American Poetry of Robert Frost would carry more command and respect in the college and could replace him.

But he was a fool because I was no threat to him, for I had no degree. Maybe I was the fool because I did not tell him the truth about my degreeless status, which would have removed the fear from his mind and given me a hold on my job.

At least, thank God, my wife did not know that I was arriving degreeless to meet joblessness. Or did she know? Judging from her letter (which I received a few days prior to my departure from New York), she was ignorant of that bit of information. Just to make certain, I opened my folder briefcase, took out her letter, and read it again as the Air India plane winged me closer to the dreaded hour.

There was no reference, not even a subtle innuendo (that is unnecessary because my wife has never been and never will be subtle) that she was aware of the loss of my job. Her letter was a long list of bring this, bring that. Some of the items asked for were for others, her friends and relatives, who had promised to pay her money.

"I have collected the money in advance. I have charged them liberally, so that when you deliver these articles, we will be making a good profit. Without making profit you cannot survive in India. Commission like corruption is compulsory for survival. Only thing, you must do it carefully and honestly, not get caught like your sister's husband," she had written.

I felt like crying, laughing, jumping up and down, and tearing the letter into shreds all at the same time.

The plane was filled to capacity, the majority being my fellow countrymen and their wives and children. Everyone seemed to be talking about all the items they were bringing or not bringing and the various ways by which they could get them through customs. Everyone seemed to have some friend, or some relative, or some relative of a friend who knew someone in the customs department who would help them out. When a few of them found out that I was not bringing anything and that I was really entitled to a certain amount of duty-free items, I became quite sought after as someone who could help them out by taking one of their items, passing it through customs as mine, and then handing it to them afterwards. I made no promises although one short guy with bad breath and body odor from Bombay was very persistent. Fortunately, when the plane landed in Bombay, there was so much confusion that I managed to get away without being further pestered by any of my countrymen to help them in their smuggling into India American-, German-, Japanese-, and Hong Kong-made goods.

I got through customs quite fast, and the moment I came out into the bright, white, hot, suffocating sunlight outside, several taxi drivers hastened to me, each one whispering that if I exchanged my foreign dollars for Indian rupees, they would give me a better exchange rate than the government. I brushed them aside and took a taxi to the railway station.

This ends my earlier letter, or Exhibit A as I said.

To continue:

I managed to get a seat on the night train to Bangalore. It was packed to overflowing capacity. I arrived in Bangalore late at night the next day. Then I waited in Bangalore for three hours for a train to Yalakki, my hometown, arriving there next evening.

There was quite a crowd of people to greet me. My mother, my in-laws, my distant and not-so-distant relatives, multitudes of children, a couple of my friends who were so young when I had left them, but who now looked old with tired faces and hair in which I thought I could detect premature streaks of gray. And of course, my wife and son leading the welcoming committee. My wife looked rounder but my son looked thinner. All of them seemed to have a garland in their hands and I thought to myself, if each of them had given me money instead, it would have helped me.

"Go on, go on," my wife urged my son, who seemed as sullen and withdrawn as he was earlier. He had a cold.

Everyone waited to garland me, and I could tell that my wife had ordered them to wait until I had been garlanded by my son. Again she urged him, while others joined in the chorus. He wiped his nose, and the mucus dripped on the garland. He seemed determined to give me a cold. I wanted to seize the garland myself and get it over with. But I forced myself to smile.

I was tired. The train journey had been quite tiring and I had had to sit up all night on the hard seat and listen to an elderly man telling me that India's spiritual heritage had the right answers to all problems and that I ought not to have gone to the West, particularly to America, although he himself had shown desire to visit America only to show the right spiritual way to all those poor Americans who have nothing *but* money. He was prepared to give them basic lessons in peace of mind in exchange for their money.

I lowered my head for my son to garland me. He only pulled back and sought refuge in the folds of my wife's sari. She pushed him toward me. He wouldn't budge. I continued to smile. Others kept saying, "Oh, he has just forgotten. Say something. He is your daddy, he has brought many exciting things for you from America."

The moment *things* were mentioned, my wife asked, "Where are all the articles, the trunks, the luggage? Were they stolen?"

"Here," I said, pointing to the two pieces of luggage at my feet.

"This is all?" she asked (rather, screamed).

"Yes. Come on, garland me, come on," I said to my son.

"Oh, they are all probably coming by separate transportation," my wife said to the crowd. I did not bother to contradict her. I merely patted my son on the back (I would have liked to slap him really) and pushed my way through the crowd to greet my mother.

She was so overwhelmed by my return that she could hardly speak. Tears gathered in her eyes. She too had aged. Then I asked, "Where is Shuba and her husband?" (Shuba is my youngest sister. It was because of her that I am married to my wife. That is a long, complicated story, to tell you another time.) No sooner had I asked that question than my mother began to sob uncontrollably, covering her mouth, wiping her eyes with the end of her sari.

I thought something disastrous had happened. "What's the matter?" I asked. That innocent question only served to increase my mother's weeping. My uncle admonished her not to weep. Others began to look upon the scene with mute despair. I looked at my wife for some sort of an explanation.

She said, "It is a very long story. I will tell you when we get home."

"Is Shuba all right?" I asked.

"As healthy as a wild donkey," my wife retorted.

I realised that it was probably some small incident that must have developed into major warfare, because in my house (ably initiated by my generalissimo wife) minor skirmishes escalate into full-blooded wars, engulfing the entire street—charges and countercharges (so and so said this, so and so said that) until the source of the irritation is forgotten and everyone is embroiled in something totally irrelevant.

I quickly turned away from this domestic squabble to greet an old friend of mine from my high school days. He smiled widely. The loss of one of his teeth made the smile even wider, but he clasped both of my hands and said: "I bring you no garland. Flowers wither, affection is forever fresh. So . . ." and had to stop his prepared speech because he broke into a fit of coughing.

Then others started greeting me, putting garlands around my neck. For a few minutes I was a hero. During those few minutes I wished I had graduated and brought home an American degree.

Various comments were made by various people. I list below a few samples:

-You have not changed at all. You are the same. We thought you would have become fat and prosperous after eating American food.

-Your skin color is the same too!

-But above all, you are your own humble self. Not proud or arrogant with your American degree from an American university.

These comments had a dual effect upon me, producing both pain and pleasure, for I knew that those who were now praising me would soon turn hostile when they got no gifts or souvenirs from me. I could hear them already: "You think I was not able to pay him? I would have. I have money. I assured him that I would pay every penny, but he's so arrogant and haughty that he did not have the courtesy to bring the item I asked for."

I also knew that the moment they discovered that I did not have a degree, they would indulge uninhibitedly (individually and collectively) in giving me a vitriol-soaked tongue-lashing: "He simply failed. Total failure, a disgrace to our whole country. Now Americans will think a dozen times before admitting an Indian student to their universities. Raja Ram Pattabhiramanna has ruined the lives of hundreds of other aspiring students."

To this charge of national disgrace that I am supposed to have brought, I will add another: "I have confidential communication from a friend of mine whose sister's son is studying in the U.S. According to that secret communication, I believe Raja Ram was actually kicked out of the university."

54

My five minutes of superstardom quickly gave way to gloom at these futuristic accusations. Right then I just wanted to go home and have some privacy (which is a rare commodity in crowded India).

My wife's first brother, a very boastful egotist, now greeted me. He was dressed gaudily in a bright, eye-blinking blue woolen suit (the temperature was 110 in the shade) with the reddest tie, knotted around a once-upon-a-time-it-was-white shirt. It had such a ring around the collar, they'd have to come up with a new detergent, for not all the Wisks in America could remove the ring around the collar of my wife's first brother. He had even put on a hat, and with his clipped Hitler moustache and oily face, he was positively both ugly and nauseating. (Add repulsive as well!)

But he had money. I guess that made him a *manmatha* (the Indian term for Adonis). True or false, about him having money, I don't know. My wife claimed that he was rich and that wealth poured into his pockets every day because he was a businessman.

Personally, I think he is like me, unemployed. He lives by his wits, like most unemployed Indians. If you ask unemployed Indians: "What are you doing?" the standard answer is: "I am in business." And if you ask: "What kind of business?" ah, there's the rub, as Hamlet would say, because there will be no specific answer. The business of looking for employment is *the* business of most people in India.

But let me not be the first person to cast the stone at the unemployed or at the vague but prestigious "cover-up" terminology (which I too must resort to, whether I like it or not).

In fact, I've decided that when the truth about my being sacked from my teaching job is known (which is bound to come out like "the murder will out" business), then to one and all who ask me: "What are you doing for your livelihood?" I will simply say: "I'm in business." After all, the real purpose in going to America was not to get a degree and return to be subservient to an ignorant and highly jealous principal; the purpose was to come back and be totally independent. I have decided to be my own boss. I am in the import and export business. I am in touch with leading American business companies and will be shipping Indian artworks, handicrafts, and so on. It will bring not only foreign exchange to our country, but it will also spread Indian culture. "Cash and Culture." I like that title. In fact I'll use it as the name of my firm. It is both practical and idealistic. I feel so relieved.

Yes, Virginia, I must actually thank you for being there in California and thereby providing me an address and an opportunity to write and express myself. It is as the result of writing to you that I am able to come up with these ideas. You are the first to know!

I also decided that I would not look down upon my ugly and overdressed brother-in-law, but rather warm up to him and learn the tricks of the trade of being in business from him.

"I have brought my car," my brother-in-law said. It was an old British car, Morris Cowley. In America this car would have been in the junkyard a long time ago. Even the junkyard (with its own standards of admission) would have rejected my brother-in-law's car. But it was his status symbol, his pride and joy.

Actually, we could all have walked to our house, not too far from the railway station. But after all is said and done, I had returned from America and people associated America with cars, so . . . anyway, to be polite, I accepted the ride. I also wanted to get away from the crowd of people. I said a general sort of "I will see you all later," to the crowd. My wife said: "They will all be at the house by the time we are there."

She was correct in this prediction (give the devil her due). It took us longer to reach my house riding in that car than they took walking. Part of the delay was caused by the fact that the car had only one openable and shuttable door. The three other doors were permanently shut with wires and rope at the door handles to keep them in place. I got in first through the front right-hand side door, sliding behind the steering wheel, and then climbing over the front seat into the backseat. But obviously, this was not the seating arrangement that my brother-in-law had in mind. As the honoured guest of his car, I was supposed to sit next to the driver, namely my brother-in-law. So I had to climb, crawl, slide, and get out so as to allow my wife to get in (which was as complicated as a camel going through the eye of the needle, or is it an elephant?—anyway, you get the picture), followed by my stubborn son, Kittu. After they got into the backseat, I urged my mother to get in.

My mother flatly refused to go though those contorted exercises and started to walk away towards our house. I mentally congratulated her on her wisdom and got in next to the driver. We had barely started (after the car had quaked and rattled) when my wife said: "You see that! Now you, yourself, are an eyewitness. I shouldn't start telling you this as soon as you have arrived (her standard opening for a long detailed report). But you see how you and my brother so kindly invited your mother to get in. Yet she said no. Now all the neighbours will see this, her walking and us in the car, and so you know what they will say? They will say, look how cruel her son and daughter-in-law are. They come like kings and queens in a car, but this elderly woman has to walk. And do you know what your mother will do? I will tell you what she will do. She will purposely start to limp as she approaches our house. And if there are a lot of neighbours watching, your mother will even sit on the side street to catch her breath, all to make me look like the cruel daughter-in-law. You know what happened three days ago? For a small matter a big fight broke out. . . ." She began laying the groundwork for another episode in the continued saga of daughter-in-law versus mother-in-law confrontation. "My brother came. He is so very busy, not even time to eat properly. See how thin he has become. Now he has so many government contracts. It is work, work all the time. . . ."

At this point my brother-in-law interrupted and said: "I do not shun work. As a matter of principle, I am against laziness."

My wife continued: "So my brother makes time for you. He came two days ago to our house. Why? So he can take me in his car to go and buy some special sweets for you upon your arrival. Can you buy these sweets just like that? No. Not these days. You must go from one restaurant to another, test and sample, to make sure the sweets are made from pure *ghee* and not rancid oil. Nowadays you cannot trust anyone, particularly restaurant owners. To make profit they will give bad health to customers and sometimes even death. Anyway, all this sweets buying took time. By the time I returned, your mother has already broadcast to all the neighbours that I am lazy, that I go out and enjoy restaurant food with my brother. One of the neighbours told me this in strictest confidence. So I determined to ask your mother directly if this was true. Instead of replying she starts to cry. I am really disgusted. So, first thing you must do is to settle this matter."

"Settle what matter?" I ask.

"What my job is and what your mother's job is. Who I should obey, you or your mother. Then one more thing about your sister. . . ."

"Let us not discuss all that now," I tried to interrupt, but that was like trying to stop fire with bare hands.

"I want to tell you my side of it before your sister and mother poison your mind," she said.

"No one will poison my mind," I told her.

"Oh, yes they will. Your own sister, your so-called favorite sister, Shuba, started weeping and left in front of everybody, making me look like a cent percent fool just twenty minutes before your train arrived this morning."

"What did you say?" I asked her.

"You see, you are also accusing me," she retorted.

"I am not accusing you. Anyway, let us discuss all this later. Is Kittu going to school regularly?" I asked, hoping to change the subject.

She ignored my question and continued: "Everyone brought garlands to garland you. Even your old friend Jayapal, in spite of his having lost his job recently in the insurance company, brought a garland. Your sister Shuba was the only one who came empty-handed. Of course your other old friend, I don't know his name, did not bring a garland. But your sister, so close to you, did not bring a garland. These things must be from the heart, not done under compulsion. Anyway, that is my opinion. I simply said, in a general way addressing all who had come but no one in particular, 'Everyone has brought garlands.' That's all I said. Suddenly your sister pounced on me, as though I had pointed her out for my remarks. She said: 'I don't have to bring any garlands for my brother, I have brought him a garland of my heart.' So I said: 'Your brother will also give you a gift of the heart, no electric hair dryer.' I know she wrote to you asking you to bring her one. So she burst into tears, even compelled your mother to go with her and not wait for your arrival. Fortunately, your mother stayed, but your sister went away weeping. So you see, I again become number one troublemaker in front of everyone. One other thing you must settle—how long your sister will stay with us. I think she and her husband are having some marriage trouble. . . ."

"She probably won't stay too long. She's got a lovely home. . . ."

"All that is gone. Her husband was dismissed because he was taking bribes right and left."

I said, "Whatever that may be, she won't stay too long with us."

"The moment you give her the electric hair dryer. . . . By the way, have you brought her the hair dryer?"

"No."

"That is good."

Fortunately, my brother-in-law said: "We will soon be at your house." The car shuddered and came to a stop in front of the third house from mine. I got out and walked back to my totally unrecognisable house.

Why my house was unrecognisable (because of my two brothers' houses, etc., etc., I have already written to you in another letter) you already know, so I will not repeat myself.

On that note, let me conclude this letter.

Further letters will follow.

> Your true love who wishes to
> see you yet does not wish to
> see you in India, and in
> Yalakki in particular,
> Raj

4

Dear, dear Virginia:

Maybe I ought not to have written you those letters with the repetitive theme (stated in a variety of forms) asking you (urging you, in fact) not to come to India.

Particularly not to Yalakki.

But if you do arrive in India, I'm sure you'll come to Yalakki (a) because you are an American and as such have boundless curiosity to know where I live, and (b) because your desire to visit Yalakki will have increased every time my letters reach you asking you not to come.

Maybe I ought to have kept quiet and thereby not created the intriguing question in your mind: "Why does Raj not want me to go to Yalakki?" Maybe I should have urged you to come to India. Frankly, I don't know which would have been the better thing.

Frankly, I'm up a wall. (Or is "up a creek" the more appropriate American expression?)

Frankly, I'm confused.

Frankly, I'm disgusted.

Yesterday evening when I returned from the post office after mailing you my letter, my wife confronted me with the dreaded question: "When are you going to your college to report back to duty?"

"I have lost my job. I have been fired." I told her without mincing words. I let her have it boldly and bluntly. In fact I enjoyed making that statement. It had the desired effect. My losing my job had a greater impact on her than upon me. Her pride suffered. I was glad.

Her waterworks started and she began to sob, not in commiseration of my loss, my symbolic loss of virility so to speak, but because she did not know how to face *her* friends, *her* relatives and *her* other assorted appendages and cronies and tell them the truth about her reduced status as the wife of an unemployed, recently-returned-from-America husband.

I added another blow. I told her I had no American degree.

Her sobs increased.

I added one more blow, deadlier than the others. I told her: "I have not brought one item you asked for, no more baggages coming by slow boat or fast plane. So you better return all the money you've collected from all those people."

Her sobbing suddenly stopped: "What shall I tell all these people who have been expecting these items?"

All these multitudes of people she should have said. Because, Virginia, from the moment I arrived, I have not had one bit of privacy. My house has had a steady stream of visitors, relatives, relatives of those relatives, friends of those relatives ad infinitum. They've crowded into every nook and cranny of my house eagerly awaiting that time when I'd distribute the gifts they've been expecting (this expectation was being constantly fueled by my wife).

My poor mother was making coffee and snacks, my wife serving them like we were running a free cafeteria. My sullen son in the meanwhile fed himself sick on the big box of chocolates I had brought, without sharing one small piece with anyone.

So when my wife asked, "What shall I tell all these people," I decided now was as good a time as any. I pushed past her, opened the door of my cubicle, and confronted the mob squeezed into my so-called living room, kitchen, etc., etc.

I clapped my hands to make them cease their endless chatter. A hush descended upon the motley crowd. Visions of tape recorders and American blenders danced in their eyes. After a brief but dramatic pause, I said: "I want all of you to leave. Get out. Leave me in peace. There is no gift for anyone. Go on, get out!"

A stunned silence followed, broken by the shrill voice of my wife's brother: "We have not come for gifts, just to see you and talk with you and learn about. . . ."

"You've seen enough of me, so leave."

My wife seized my arm to calm me down. I pulled away. The gathering of the greedy began to dissolve. I knew they'd mumble and mutter: "He's drunk. Took up the habit in America. We may not have gone to America but at least we have good morality and ancient tradition," and so on and so forth.

Who cares? I couldn't take it anymore. So in my own way, I too had chased the money changers away from the temple like Oliver Cromwell dissolving the Parliament. I think you get the general idea, don't you, Virginia?

So much for the most recent happening.

In a few days I'll write again.

> Until then,
> Your sweetheart in spirit and
> thought,
>
> Raj

5

CASH AND CULTURE
A New Concept in Culture Export

Telephone: India Office:
Cable: CACU   9¹/₂ Jasmine Alley
                               Yalakki
R. R. Raj, President   Karnataka State
                               India
                               U.S. Office:
                               2222 Laurel Drive
                               Avalon, California 90704
                               U.S.A.

Dear Virginia:

Well, here it is. My new stationery. What do you think of it? Be candid, honest. I want the blunt, naked truth.

I have applied for a telephone (or will be applying for one soon), and when the telephone is sanctioned (God knows when), I will simply type the numbers next to where it says "Telephone." The cable is purely for decorative purposes. So don't try to cable me, for it is nonexistent, and to be honest with you, I have no immediate intentions of getting that cable address.

I have, I admit, taken undue liberties in using your address as my U.S. office. But my only excuse is that I have taken you at your word: "If I can help in any way, feel free to call on me." Your words to me as we had coffee and apple pie in Hacienda, that restaurant on Hollywood Boulevard in Los Angeles, a month before I left for Yalakki.

Again, using your address is purely decorative. Consider it my substitution for the American degree which I did not obtain. It is a way of letting my customers know that I have contacts in America, even if it is one contact and it is you. If it is good and reliable, one contact is enough. And, Virginia, you are good, you are reliable, you are my lifeline.

With the printing of this stationery (500 sheets), I have temporarily silenced my innumerable relatives, including my loudmouthed, tart-tongued wife, from asking their impertinent, meddling, nagging question: "What are your plans?"

My plans are to earn cash through the spread of culture.

I flash my calling card (same contents as the print on my stationery, but I am enclosing a sample so you'll know) and both surprise and silence them.

Do you know that I am really beginning to enjoy writing these letters to you. It is like talking with you. I mean it in a very literal sense. So even if you do not reply to my letters, and even if nothing comes out of it (not that I'm expecting anything out of it), I have decided to continue writing letters until . . . something happens, whatever that something may be.

I think I will keep copies of my letters from this letter onward. If it is possible and not too much trouble, please get me a photocopy of my earlier letters—three or four, I don't quite remember at the moment. I can of course check from my diary. But my diary is' in a trunk, and the trunk along with my other things is on the veranda and I do not want to get up and go to the veranda to get it because that simple act of looking into my diary might upset my present flow of thought. Further, I might run into my brother-in-law who is still hanging around my house, feeding all kinds of illusions of glory to my wife. I am sure that he is just outside listening to the noise of this typewriter, and that noise will give him some hesitancy in encroaching on my privacy, which I miss most and hence cherish most since my arrival back in India.

I have managed to steal some privacy by telling my wife that she or anyone else must not disturb me while I am typing. Of course, don't for one moment think that *that* simple statement makes her obey me. Oh no, she had a series of questions as to what I was typing, why the privacy, and whether I was spending time in corresponding with Lynda Ginda (Ginda is not her last name, by the way).

Lynda was the graduate student at Avalon College with whom I spent a few minutes one evening in the library lounge. We had been sitting innocently that evening and for some strange reason I was smoking that day. I don't really smoke, but that day when Lynda offered me a cigarette, I simply took it. She lit it, and I must have taken just one puff. But I was holding it with the smoke curling up. Again, for some reason I do not quite know, something happened in the conversation between Lynda and me. I think I said, "Oh no, I don't believe it," and we laughed uproariously. At that precise moment my wife made her entrance and started lambasting me openly. Fortunately, there were just two of us in the lounge. My wife went on accusing me, alternating her accusations between Kannada and English, switching to Kannada whenever she wanted to be more offensive. "Your son is about to die from stomachache and you are carrying on with this American girl," and so on and so forth. Lynda finally excused herself and left.

Well, my wife has never forgotten that incident. Whenever her arguments fail, she refers to that incident . . . followed by great weeping and what not . . . as with the loss of my job at the college here. "You were busy with that Lynda Ginda, that is why you did not write properly to the college principal, so he fired you."

By the way, whenever my wife refers to Lynda it is always done in a rhythmic way, like Lynda Ginda. That is part of her thinking in Kannada, because most people when they speak (especially if it is disparaging) have that habit. Like those who want to be sarcastic towards me will always say: "Oh, you are a big man, you have been to America Gimerica," or they'll never simply ask if you will have some coffee. It is always: "Will you have some coffee geefy?" and so on. So my wife always has this standard response: "You failed to get a degree in America because you were so busy with that Lynda Ginda. You did not bring all the articles I asked you to bring because of spending your money on that Lynda Ginda."

When I complained of my need for privacy, she immediately retorted: "Just as I expected. Oh, yes, you want to sit and think about that Lynda Ginda and probably keep looking at her picture."

I told her that I was going to write a book about India. If I did that, I could send it to a publisher and get a lot of money. The moment she knew that there was going to be some money as a result of my privacy, she agreed to keep away. But this meant that if I should have privacy, I must be producing typing sounds. I thought I could just get inside this room and be by myself, but that was not possible because three minutes after I closed the door, she was in. The following conversation took place:

ME: Go away.
SHE: But you are not typing.
ME: I am thinking.
SHE: For that you don't need privacy.
ME: Why?
SHE: If you are seriously thinking about something, then you can do it in the noisiest railway station, like thinking about God. I can be in a crowded temple with babies crying, coconuts being broken, the priest chanting mantras, people wandering about, but when I close my eyes and think of God, I hear no sounds except the Heavenly music. So. . . .
ME: Maybe you can do it, I can't.
SHE: That is just an excuse. You just want to waste your time by saying you want privacy. For typing you may need privacy because you have to look at the typewriter and type with your one finger, and with no privacy you make mistakes, but for thinking you don't need privacy.

From then on it became certain that if I needed privacy, I had better keep producing those typing sounds. I wish that instead of this one cassette of Bob Dylan songs I brought for that small portable cassette player, which I sent home with my wife, I had bought an hour-long cassette with the sounds of someone typing. I could have slipped it in and let it play and thus had my privacy without having to sit and type when I could have been thinking. I cannot ask you to send it even if there were such a cassette—typing sounds for moments of privacy—because any gift coming from overseas would be very difficult to get in.

Unfortunately I am not an American. If I were I would have devised one of those instant inventions like the Roadrunner does in those foolish but joyous cartoons to catch the crafty fox or whatever the other animal is that is driving the Roadrunner crazy. A rope tied to my foot and tied to the typewriter would do, so that by moving my foot casually I could produce the clickety click of the typewriter to keep my wife away. (Better title for the cassette: Typing Sounds to Keep Your Wife Away!!!)

Believe me, it is quite torturous, this whole thing. So much for now, Virginia. I will write again. In the meantime I will go on just typing the ???????? to symbolise my life on sheet after sheet to produce the sounds to get me privacy.

Your one and only true love,
Raj

6

Dear Virginia,

How welcome it is to get your letter, but alas too brief. You are very parsimonious with your words. But the fact that you've received all my letters (I assume, because you don't mention how many. So please confirm. According to my count I have written you 5 letters, 6 if you include this one.)

I am glad that you found my letters to be "a lot of fun" and that "Jeff got a great big kick out of them. He read parts of them loudly and broke up."

Jeff is your brother, am I right? (Your kid brother, as you used to refer to him? The one who was into the "meditation yoga bit," which "bit" he entered into after leaving behind his "beach bum surfer bit." And then the one time you said: "He'll soon get over the India bit too. It's a phase that American teenagers pass through, like acne.") If my memory serves me right (and all I have now to sustain me are memories of my wonderful stay in America!), then these above comments are the only ones you've made about your kid brother.

If Jeff takes after you, then he must be a very stunningly handsome youth.

Has he passed through the "India meditation yoga bit" and into some other bit now?

Is it asking too much if I were to ask you to tell me what bit he is into? It is of little bits and pieces that we seem to be made up anyway.

My letters were to you, Virginia, to you PERSONALLY, not for displaying to your kid brother for him to read loudly and get a big kick out of them. Or am I to assume that your brother is now into the reading-other-people's-letters-to-get-a-kick-out-of-them bit?

I seem to have no privacy anywhere. Not in India, and it looks like I don't have it in America either. I am in my letters! In other words, I AM WHAT I WRITE. If you want to know the real truth, my writing to you was a result of my deep hunger for privacy, to share with you and you alone my innermost thoughts. But you have shared them with your kid brother who might want to share them with his buddies to give them the pleasure of getting a kick out of my letters.

I can almost hear him saying to his marijuana-smoking, jean-clad, sneaker-shod, sweat-suffused, long-haired, wine-drinking buddies: "My sister's got this weirdo who writes these kooky letters, all the way from India. Listen to this . . ." and then reading excerpts from my letters. I can hear the raucous laughter that greets these words that I've torn from my guts to place before you, my sweetheart. Then they'll probably form a rock group and set my letters to music and make a million (my private thoughts sold for the all-mighty dollar!).

There you have it, my naked reaction to your letter. The scornful laughter of your kid brother and his buddies rings shrilly in my ears and I reread your phrase, "lot of fun," and wonder if you too joined in that scornful laughter.

But, I am what I am. I shall continue to write, continue to share my thoughts with you. Don't share my letters with your kid brother Jeff. Please. Enough of that. . . .

My brother-in-law has proven himself to be an obnoxious person. He is not to be trusted. (Can anyone be trusted? I ask but will not wait for an answer.) You know what happened? Of course you don't, so let me tell you.

I had exactly 120 dollars in traveller's checks when I arrived at my doorstep in India. I had to cash 20 dollars right away for some incidental expenses. That one hundred dollars plus the three cubby-holes of my so-called house were all that constituted my so-called assets. In anticipation of the articles my wife assumed I would bring from America, she had (with her usual unlimited greed) collected money from various people. Further, she was so confident that I would bring these items that she had gone ahead and spent thirty dollars of the amount she had collected. When the bare-bones truth struck her, that I was not joking, that there would be no packages with gifts coming, she confided to me that she had spent money from the money she'd collected, but that she had done it for me!

Demands for return of that spent money poured in, and I had no other choice but to take care of it. I went to the bank and cashed the thirty dollars to pay off the folly of my wife.

The next day my brother-in-law stops by, ostensibly to give me a ride to the bank in his car so that I can cash the remaining checks. I decline his offer. He is persistent. I succumb. He grins. We go.

On the way (pedestrians walk faster than my brother-in-law's car goes) he unravels his sinister scheme. He knows of someone who is prepared to give me six times the government exchange rate for my precious dollars. I resist. He persists. I put up all kinds of arguments from patriotism to pure ethics. He breaks each of my arguments with the simple statement: "You are jobless, you need all the money you can get to establish your new business on a sound footing."

I succumb. Poverty is the root of all evil, not money. That is my humble opinion, Virginia.

I sign on the line where it says: countersignature. I hand over to my brother-in-law six ten-dollar checks. I keep one ten-dollar check back. "You are doing the right thing," he says, grinning from ear to ear and showing off his betel-leaves-stained teeth. "You see, by taking my advice you have already increased your original investment. If you know how to go about making money, you can make as much money as Americans make."

But I tell him that Americans do not indulge in such petty methods.

"They do it on a bigger scale," he says, "but whether they do it or not, in India, do as Indians do." We drive to a restaurant. He asks me to wait, orders me a special coffee with cream, and disappears inside the restaurant to transact the shady deal, probably in the smoky kitchen.

One hour later (no exaggeration, Virginia! exactly one hour later) he returns with a harried expression, and mopping his forehead, urges me to leave. In almost a whisper he says: "Pay for that coffee and come on," and rushes out of the restaurant.

I obey and join him.

He starts to speak only after we have driven for about a half-hour. "We escaped by the breath of our hair. In these days you cannot trust anyone, not even your best friend. A trap had been set. The purchaser of the traveller's check was a government agent. You must thank me. I saved you from going to prison."

Then he dropped the bombshell which in a sense I expected him to drop: "I had to use all my skill in arguments plus a bribe of your sixty dollars in traveller's checks to save you from disgrace and going to prison. We are poor, but no one in our entire family has ever gone to prison. What disgrace it would have brought on us all. How would my sister react to it? She might even have committed suicide. . . ."

"Just shut up," I said.

He did that, but only for a while. "I know you need the money and if I may offer you a suggestion. . . ."

"You want me to take another loss? No! All I have is ten dollars. I should never have listened to you in the first place," I said.

But I was a captive audience in his one-door car, even *that* effectively blocked by him in the driver's seat.

So he offered me a suggestion: to pawn my wife's jewelry and get some money to launch my business. "You will only be pawning it, not selling it. After all, what is the purpose of jewelry if it's not meant to be used in times of need?" he continued on and on.

"Your sister, namely my wife, will never agree to part with her jewelry," I said (which incidentally consisted of one gold necklace worth five sovereigns or three and a half ounces of gold and two bangles worth two ounces of gold. Like most Indian women, my wife had kept these away, hidden, wearing them only at festivals or to impress someone, the latter being the reason for their purchase in the first place).

"Not to worry about that, I already have it with me," he said.

"You have it?" I asked.

"For safekeeping. My sister is suspicious of your sister, Shuba, and therefore she, that is *my* sister, gave the jewelry to me for safe-keeping."

I was bristling with anger so much that I could hardly find the words. He seized my tongue-tied state and continued.

I succumbed, because I needed the money and also to teach my wife a lesson.

My brother-in-law stopped the car. He got out, lifted the old worn-out seat on which he had been sitting. Beneath some old newspaper he had hidden the jewelry in a very dirty handkerchief which he handed to me. He got back in the car, and we drove to a Marwari moneylender's shop, two hours distant.

When we reached the shop, I firmly told my brother-in-law that I wanted to be present at the transaction. He readily agreed, saying he needed me to sign the pawn document.

The conniving moneylender with his mountainous belly, enormous drooping soup-strainer moustache, and his constant belching examined the jewelry (with total disdain) and offered me a ridiculously small amount with a 25 percent interest rate. The haggling began.

My brother-in-law hastily joined in the battle of wits. We haggled and then decided to leave. The moneylender relented. We agreed. Finally, I received a thousand rupees minus 25 percent (interest for first year deducted in advance) and headed home.

Next day my brother-in-law demanded his pound of flesh. He wanted a loan from me. (Out of the money I'd gotten from the moneylender.)

Giving a loan to my brother-in-law would be like kissing money good-bye! I flatly refused. He bluntly called out my wife and told her (that double-crossing scoundrel) that I had stolen her jewelry and pawned it.

All hell broke loose!

She screamed, shouted, and wept, egged on by my brother-in-law. My mother, sister, and other assorted relatives from my family side began to support me. Thus began a shouting, screaming match.

The ridiculous absurdity of the situation overwhelmed me. I could take it no more and began to laugh hysterically. I became uncontrollable. I was in one of those clutching-your-stomach-body-

convulsing-tears and laughter-mingling body-aching laughter outbursts! The shouting and screaming stopped. The walls resounded to
my laughter. Everyone thought I had gone mad. One by one they left.
I howled. I wanted to stop but I could not. It was as though invisible
fingers were tickling me.

But I was left alone. A semblance of peace returned.

Now I am left alone. Food is left outside my room.

But is this life? I ask myself. Because, Virginia, beneath all this
Rabelaisian, rambunctious laughter is a vale of tears too deep for
words.

I prepare myself carefully before I come out of the room, to go
to the bathroom, or for any other compulsive bodily demands, and
burst into laughter the second I emerge. Immediately a way is cleared
for me, and even if there is a long line in front of the bathroom or
wherever, it disperses quickly.

But my laughter is wearing thin. Yesterday it took a long time,
quite a long time to work up laughter before emerging from the room.
And then it did not last long. To be frank, I was on the verge of tears,
and when I returned to my room broke into uncontrollable sobs.

There is some kind of frantic activity going on in the house. One
thing I know, my wife, aided by that ugly, shady, double-crossing,
backbiting, deceitful brother of hers, is consulting some astrologer. I
think he will suck them dry. Astrologers are as bad as lawyers. My
only consolation is that since my wife has no money, her brother
might come to her rescue and thereby be sucked dry by this astrologer,
who incidentally used to be a lawyer. So, he is a doubly dangerous
character. He used to wear white trousers, white shirt, black tie, and
black jacket, with a starched, gold-bordered white turban—typical
dress of an Indian lawyer. Now he has shoulder-length hair and a
luxuriant beard. Western dress has been replaced by a simple white
dhoti and a loose, knee-length white shirt. He wears a beaded necklace and his forehead is boldly decorated with three imposing horizon-
tal ash stripes. He has lost weight, and his cadaverous appearance has
given him a strange, otherworldly, half-dead look. I know he is a
fraud, a sham, a bogus, but my wife worships him. He thinks I don't
know who he is, but I know who he was, and who he is. He has ruined

many lives through dragged-out litigation proceedings. Now he wants to drag people through extraterrestrial planetary proceedings. Bloodsuckers, the whole damn rotten bunch.

But my wife believes in all these characters. Maybe I should have been an astrologer or an artificial holy man to win her respect, maybe then I could have controlled her. It is all very muddled up anyway.

Well, Virginia, all I can say is I am on the verge of making a major decision. What it is, I don't know. Not as yet. But decide I will, *that* decision I have made.

Your few letters are much too short.

Yours,
Raj

7

Dear Virginia:

A very, very important matter. Each and every time I have written to you, I have wanted to mention something very, very important, but for one reason or the other (too much on my mind), I have forgotten to. So, before I forget it again, let me mention it.

Do you remember the notebook wrapped in brown paper and marked confidential, personal property of Raja Ram, that I gave you for safekeeping just before my departure to India?

You asked me: "What is this?"

I said: "A very controversial literary work, bound to be banned in India if it is ever published."

"Oh, how exciting. Can I read it?" you asked.

"Please not now. Please promise that you will not open it and read it," I requested.

"At least tell me what it is. Is it a novel, play, a collection of . . ." you started.

"It is a combination of several things. A sort of private journal. It is called 'Secret Whispers,'" I said.

"Sounds pornographic," you said.

"Not pornographic, rather sensuous," I said.

Virginia, I know that you have not read the notebook ("Secret Whispers"). You have made no reference to it in any of your letters. I assume you have it tucked away in some safe secret place and have forgotten about it. It is good if you have forgotten about it, but I hope you will remember where you put it! Anyway, Virginia, thank you for keeping it.

I thank you for respecting my privacy. I am ready to believe that your sharing my letters with your kid brother Jeff was purely an accident. I am prepared to forget that invasion of my privacy.

I want to renew my request, Virginia. Please retain that package containing "Secret Whispers." Please do not read it. I am planning some strategy to have it returned to me. More on that later.

Thank you, Virginia, thank you,

As ever,

Raj

P.S.: I learn that my house will become even more crowded within the very near future. My two brothers who were unable to come to Yalakki to welcome me when I returned from America because they are working and living in different parts of the country, are expected to descend upon my house, accompanied by their wives and children. My two sisters are also expected, of course with their husbands and their children. All this because of my mother's summons to them. She is convinced that I am really mad. My wife has also summoned her younger brother to arrive with his wife and (naturally) their children. The battle forces are gathering. I dread the thought of being here when the gathering of the clan takes place. I know I will be right dead center in the eye of the hurricane. I can only borrow the words of the Irish poet, William Butler Yeats, and say, "Things are falling apart, the center cannot hold." Of course these may not be his exact words, but you get the general idea.

I have made a decision to make a decision. What I will do, when I will do it, how I will do it, where I will do it, I know not at this time. But do I will. I must.

Do I make any sense at all?

How I wish you were close by, Virginia. Yes, that is my dear wish, for you to be close by. Close enough for me to visit you, but difficult for you to visit me. Does that make any sense? I am sure it raises the question to your mind: "Why does Raj not want me to go to Yalakki?"

The answer is obvious to someone as intelligent as you. Where would I even find a comfortable seat for you to sit? There is absolutely no privacy at all for heart-to-heart conversations. My wife would play to the hilt her role of the jilted wife and I would become the despicable adulterer. She would script a scenario that I'm stringing along two women, one domestic and the other foreign.

So I do not want you to come. Not for now anyway. Let us therefore, dear Virginia, be the star-cross'd lovers till better times arrive.

> Yours in excruciatingly
> painful dilemma,
> Raj

PART THREE

○　○　○

HOLY MAN

1

VIRGINIA'S STORY

Raja Ram came only slowly into my life—though in the end he was more of a walking fireworks display than a friend or acquaintance. I had seen him on the Avalon campus, and I knew he was from India and that he had a wife and son.

Then one evening I saw him at the library. He was working at the front entrance desk, examining books to make sure they had been checked out.

"Oh, you are interested in reincarnation?" he asked in a pleasant, singsong voice, looking at the book in my hand.

"Yes, I am. In fact . . ." I wondered if I should ask him straight out. Then I thought, why not? "I was thinking of getting in touch with you to ask if you'd be interested in speaking to our group one evening."

"On reincarnation?"

"Yes. You're from India, aren't you?"

"Yes, but that does not necessarily make me an authority on reincarnation. However, I believe in it," he said.

"Well, how about just talking to us about why you believe in it, what your reasons are?"

"My belief is based more on faith, less on reason."

"That's even better. Articulating your faith is sometimes harder than giving it a rationale; at least that's what Professor Rawlins thinks. Would you be willing to?"

"You are very persuasive, if I may say so," he said smiling. "What is the name of your group?"

"We don't have a name. We're not really even organized. About a dozen of us meet at Professor John Rawlins's house every couple of weeks on Thursday evenings. Do you know Professor Rawlins?"

"No."

"He teaches philosophy. He's very interested in India, particularly Indian philosophy. He's planning to write a book on it."

"I should be most interested in meeting him."

"I'm surprised he hasn't been in touch with you already."

"Perhaps I have been keeping a low profile, as your president says." He smiled and I smiled back. "So you meet and talk about intellectual matters?"

"Not always so intellectual. A month ago we spent the whole evening discussing pornographic symbolism in soap operas."

"Pornographic?"

"I promise we'll be very serious when we discuss reincarnation," I said.

"I'm not as serious as I look," he said.

"Good. We're very informal. Whatever you want to talk about we'll enjoy. Will you do it?"

"How can I say no, when you are so charming and friendly?"

"Good. I'll check with Professor Rawlins and get back to you. By the way, I'm Virginia Gleason. Just call me Ginny."

"I'm Raj for short."

"Short for what?"

"Well . . . Raja Ram Pattabhiramanna," he said slowly with several pauses.

"I'll settle for the short one, Raj," I said and laughed.

That's how I met him. The proposed talk and discussion on reincarnation never took place. I can't remember why. But Raj and I became friends. He even talked to me about his marital problems, including some revelations about embarrassing, rather intimate details, which I did not invite. Then his wife and son returned to India and he changed noticeably, became more relaxed and, in fact, quite charming. He had a good sense of humor and a way of saying things that made you (or at least me) want to hug him sometimes. I helped him give a party at his apartment once, and we took some trips together to San Francisco, Carmel, Los Angeles, and San Diego. I enjoyed his company. But Raj never seemed to be able to apply himself to anything effectively, so his academic work suffered. When it got really bad, the college decided not to renew his financial aid. I'm not sure what the problem was. He seemed restless, filled with schemes, always intent on pursuing something irrelevant to anything else in his life. It was ironic; he spent much of his time trying to figure out how to stay in America permanently and neglected what was necessary—his studies—to maintain the student status he already had. He even talked about going underground and becoming an illegal immigrant, but that would have been really crazy. So he returned to India.

I saw him off at the airport. "Keep in touch, will you," I said, feeling very warm toward him. "I'd love to hear from you, so please write." Little did I know what I was letting myself in for. Actually, I rather missed him at first and so took the initiative in starting the correspondence. I wrote him several times, but didn't hear back until, suddenly, the dam broke and the flood of letters began.

I couldn't tell whether he thought of me as a romantic interest or not while he was here in Avalon. He never made any overt approaches, though he enjoyed touching in ways that were almost, but not quite, intimate. It was only after he got back to India that he declared his love in those long, screwball letters, and then I had to take them with a grain of salt.

My own feelings were ambivalent. My life was too complicated for an affair at that time, and I don't know if Raj would have been the person anyway. I think he saw me as a love that might have been, which he could idealize and then use as a defense against the life he had to return to in India. Maybe to some degree I did the same thing.

I know I enjoyed his wacky letters. They opened a window on a world so totally different from my own and so bizarre, as seen through Raj's eyes, that I found myself eagerly awaiting them and reading them avidly as soon as they arrived.

But with my graduate studies, my work as part-time reporter for *The Avalon Clarion,* and nursing my seventy-two-year-old arthritic mother who was suffering from a hip injury, there was no way I could keep up with him.

I acknowledged most of his letters, wrote brief replies, promised him longer letters "next time," sympathized with his readjustment problems, and casually suggested that if he felt so trapped, he ought to think of returning to the U.S., though I didn't know how he'd do it with his poor academic record at Avalon.

Then he abruptly stopped writing.

I missed his letters, as did my brother Jeff, who got a charge out of reading them loudly in a flawless imitation of Raj's singsong accent, complete with hand gestures and facial expressions, which was incredible because Jeff had met Raj just once very briefly. I had not shown Jeff those letters. He came across them quite by accident and even attempted to photocopy them without my knowledge! Raj was very angry when I told him about it, which I could kick myself for doing, although I also felt a little guilty about encouraging Jeff to do his act, once he had access to them. Jeff could be very puerile as a teenager.

Then out of the blue, I received a letter from Raj's wife, Vimala. It was a curious coincidence because I was just about to write to Raj to see if he wanted a job assisting Professor Rawlins in some research he was planning to do in India on his book. It was a long, rambling letter stating that Raj had disappeared. Vimala had consulted a reliable astrologer "of international reputation" and he told her that I had lured Raj away from her. She wanted me to return her husband immediately! If I failed to do so, she would take legal action and the astrologer would take spiritual action against me.

I replied by return mail, saying that Raj was not with me and that I had no inkling of his whereabouts. I speculated that he might have just taken off for a short period to think things over and asked her to drop me a line when he returned. I was certain Raj's disappearing act was one of his tricks, to create a sense of shock in his wife, like his deviously improvised typing sounds or hysterical bursts of laughter to secure his privacy. Maybe his disappearance was the major decision he had talked about in his last letter to me.

I expected to hear from Raj any day and to have him describe in minute detail where he was and what he was doing. Instead, I got a continuous stream of letters from Vimala—all variations on the same theme as her first letter. She remained unconvinced of my innocence and regarded me with conviction as the femme fatale behind her marital tragedy.

Her letters were funny in a morbid sort of way, and also a little frightening in their intensity. "Why do you want to steal my husband when there are so many beautiful, strong, well-educated, and rich American men? What do you see in my husband? In our culture divorce is not natural like it is in yours. We are married for life. Do you know how much shame I am facing in my community? Everyone is saying that I drove my husband away. So, like one woman to another woman, please understand the storm in my heart and use all your force to return my husband," she wrote in one letter.

I replied, emphasizing over and over that I had no knowledge of Raj's whereabouts. I assured her that if Raj were indeed in the U.S. and if I came across any information about him, I would cable her. In the meanwhile I wished her good luck and joined in her prayers for Raj's swift and safe return.

That did not satisfy her. Her letters continued, filled with dark hints of drastic steps she would take to end her life if I did not come out with the truth and inform the Immigration Service so they could deport Raj. Some of the letters contained crude sketches of a noose over a well, of a hooded cobra, and a funeral pyre in flames. They upset me a great deal, and I wished she would stop writing. I began to have nightmares about her committing suicide. In one, Raj's son appeared and accused me of driving his mother to jump into the waterless well which housed the hooded cobra at the end of the street where they lived. I woke up with a scream, sweating.

After this, I tore up her letters as they arrived without reading them. Without my response, the letters gradually decreased in number and finally stopped.

In the meantime John Rawlins's life was disrupted because a series of misfortunes plunged him into despair. His marriage to Maggie broke up, and then after that he had an automobile accident which resulted in the loss of his left leg. And I had my own problems also. Professor Rawlins was my master's thesis advisor, so my work had to be slowed down. In addition, my mother's condition took a turn for the worse, and since she obstinately refused to enter a nursing home, my hands were full taking care of her. In the midst of all this upheaval, Raj faded from my memory.

I thought of him briefly when I got a letter from my brother Jeff. Instead of going straight to college from high school, he took off with his friend Chris to wander—"bumming" he called it—around the world for a while (which turned out to be several years!). He wrote to me from Bangkok, saying he was headed for India. He wanted the address of "that kooky friend of yours who used to write those funny letters to you," so that he and his friend could crash at Raj's place for a few days. Jeff also said he'd taken Raj's journal, "Secret Whispers," which he had found in the upstairs trunk where I had hidden it. "I didn't mean to take it with me, but I lent it to Chris and he brought it along, thought it would be a good 'orientation' to our trek through India. Boy, is it hot stuff! Did you read it? Raja Ram, with the long unpronounceable name, Yalakki's own Rudy Valentino. He's something! If you'll give me his address, I'll wrap it up the way it was and hand deliver it to him. He probably won't know the difference."

I felt both envious and infuriated with Jeff, envious that he was enjoying himself while I was tied down and getting older by the day, infuriated that he should have taken Raj's book without so much as asking my permission. I did not reply to him, and even if I had, I would not have given him Raj's address. As far as I knew, Raj wasn't even there. Also, with all the problems Raj had, I did not want to burden him with the appearance of two insensitive ugly Americans (though I learned later that Chris, who was the more obnoxious of the two, dropped out in Bangkok so that Jeff arrived in Yalakki alone).

The months passed. My mother became completely bedridden and, after much persuasion, moved to a nursing home. John Rawlins and I, commiserating with each other, grew close. It wasn't the affair of my dreams, though it was warm, caring, and gentle. I sometimes wondered if Raj would have been the right man ... but not often. He was too far off in La La Land for me.

John continued to work on his book which was about the impact the new exotic religions—the Moonies, the Hare Krishnas, and others—were having on American youngsters. There'd been a rash of books, newspaper articles, and TV reports on the subject, and John was a little discouraged. "There's nothing new to say," he told me one day, "especially if I can't do the research I need to do in India." But I encouraged him to continue, if only because it would be good therapy, though I didn't say that to him.

"Look," I said, "you're doing something different. You're studying the minds and psyches of the messiahs behind these religions, getting inside their heads, finding out what drives them, and you don't have to have the India research to do it. You've been researching Indian philosophy twenty years." That wasn't quite true, but it sounded good. "Hey, I think there's a good chance you'll have a smash hit. How about eight weeks on the *New York Times* best-seller list and a six-figure contract for the paperback rights?"

To help keep him moving, I started working for him—organizing his research data and handling details that annoyed him, like answering the phone. It was at this point that I heard from Thelma Neilson. Oddly, she was calling John to find me when I picked up the phone in his office.

I won't go into detail on our conversation. Thelma is a dear chatterbox with more enthusiasm for doing good than anyone I've ever known. She's very lightweight, but fun—at least she was when I was in contact with her, which was when Raj was in Avalon. It was nice to hear her voice.

We reminisced for a bit, especially about the party I helped Raj give—actually, we both helped him. Raj had invited fifty people and had enough food for about five! Vimala would have been horrified; she'd have cooked enough for a hundred!

"I remember you rushed out and brought back several buckets of Kentucky Fried," Thelma said.

"I kept telling him, we've got to have more food. But he kept saying, 'The food's very hot, very spicy, most people will come just to have a taste of Indian food . . . don't you think?' I'm as bad as Jeff imitating his accent that way. But you saved the day with your potato salad and cream pies," I said. "I thought you were a magician."

Then Thelma got down to business. She was calling about Raj.

"Have you heard from him recently?" I asked.

"Yes, from both of them." There was a pregnant silence.

"Vimala, too, huh?" I said, not very enthusiastically.

"Is that a problem?"

"Well . . . no, I guess not." I didn't really want to stir that up inside me again.

"In fact, I've *seen* them."

"Really? Where?"

"In India."

Well, it turned out that Goody-Two-Shoes, as Jeff called Thelma, had signed up for an India tour sponsored by the American Business and Professional Women's Association. It was a two-week program of strenuous and serious travel; they conducted interviews with professional women all over India (so much for the goody-two-shoes image), and Thelma managed to squeeze in two days in Yalakki.

"Is Raj back?" I asked.

"Indeed, he is," she said with a laugh.

I tried to get her to describe her experiences, but she said she didn't have time and didn't want to until she sent two letters she had received—one from Raj and one from Vimala—which would pretty much tell the whole story.

"I'll be back in touch after you've had a chance to read them."

I hung up, curious, and with a very strong sense of anticipation, much stronger than I would have expected. Strange how Raja Ram had worked himself under my skin.

Three days later I received Thelma's large envelope with the two letters. I decided to read Raj's letter first.

2

Dear Mrs. Neilson:

Where to begin? How to begin? What words to begin with?

Let me begin with a profound apology. I ask your forgiveness from the bottom of my heart. Sincerely, devoutly.

Here you are, a devoted friend—no, you are more than a friend. You are practically like a mother. You put yourself through great inconvenience to come to this small postage-stamp-size of a town by the name of Yalakki. You come to visit me with friendship and affection.

What do I do?

I frighten you in the dead of the night. I make you scream and cry for help. Then I run away like a thief in the night to save my skin. That was not my intention when I entered your room. I am ashamed. I am embarrassed.

Sorry, sorry, sorry, a thousand times. I ask your generous forgiveness.

I earnestly hope that this letter, which is undoubtedly the single most important letter I have ever written or will ever write, will reach you. I beg you to reply to me at your earliest, with the phrase "I understand, I forgive" incorporated in the body of the thank-you-for-your-warm-hospitality letter you are bound to write my wife from America. I have my own method of finding out if your letter has reached my wife. If the above words, namely, "I understand, I forgive" are in that letter, then I will have some temporary peace of mind.

Friday, March 23, that night of infamy in Yalakki, will forever be etched in my mind and heart as a day of personal shame and disgrace.

I entered your room, not to frighten you but to explain my strange and bizarre situation to you, face to face. I came to tell you how due to a series of circumstances, I had worked myself into a mess. I came to ask your help to get me out of it. The dark, moonless night, the ghostly white robe I wore gave me an eerie, otherworldly appearance. Naturally such an image scared you. Thus, instead of eliciting your friendly, full-of-smiles "Hello, Raj, I am delighted to see you" greeting, you were compelled to scream, "Help, help! A burglar!" A tragedy of errors.

I wanted to place my hand on your mouth to assure you that I was harmless. Thank God I did not do that. I might have given you a heart attack. What a calamity that would have been.

I am not exactly certain what happened after I fled. I heard a variety of conflicting stories the next day. Bits and fragments. Most of it fabricated out of rumours and gossip and grossly exaggerated accounts of how a wealthy American woman had been robbed of hundreds of dollars. It became the hottest news in Yalakki. It is being discussed even now. Several have tried to consult me in secrecy to find out if I could, through my special powers, help locate the allegedly stolen dollars. The hotel manager, that big, fat-bellied Mukundappa, has emerged as a hero for having saved your life. I could have questioned my wife about what you did after I fled, and attempted to worm out such information as when and how you departed from Yalakki. But on careful reflection, I decided not to probe my wife, remembering the old but nevertheless true proverb, "Curiosity killed a cat." Also, my wife would not have given me an accurate report. I have reason to believe that she wanted to use your visit as an opportunity to humiliate me. More on that later in the course of this letter.

Outwardly I have maintained an attitude of total indifference concerning the unfortunate incident on that night of Friday, March 23. But inwardly my heart cries out in deep sorrow and anguish for my repulsive behavior towards a dear and good friend, a veritable mother, whose help and affection I can never forget as long as I live.

Again, please forgive me.

When I heard that you were coming to India and that Madras was one of the stops in your travel plans, I knew you would make every effort to visit Yalakki. I had mixed feelings about your impending visit. On the one hand, I wanted you to come. I wanted to welcome you to Yalakki about which I had spoken so much when I was in Avalon. "Raja Ram is from India and describes his hometown of Yalakki, which incidentally means *cardamom* (an Indian spice plant of the ginger family with seeds used as a condiment and in medicine), as a quiet little town nestling by a gently flowing river, far from the madding crowd's ignoble strife." Do you remember that sentence from the college newspaper? I am sure you do, because when you first called me up to invite me to speak to your group, you introduced yourself and said, "I love the way you've described your hometown. I love Thomas Hardy." Then you read the sentence from the college newspaper. I remember it well. What glorious days they were in Avalon!

The news about your impending visit brought back such nostalgic memories. I yearned to talk with you heart to heart. But because of the plots-within-plots drama which is being enacted in Yalakki and into which I have (unwittingly and unintentionally) stumbled as an actor, I realized with a sad heart that I would be unable to welcome you and indulge in the rare luxury of such a talk.

Much has happened since you last saw me in Avalon. Since you were not in Avalon the day I left San Francisco to catch my flight to New York en route to India, I was deprived of the pleasure of saying good-bye to you personally and thanking you for your many gestures of friendship and also for the thoughtful gift of a box of homemade chocolate fudge. I asked Virginia Gleason (I think you remember her from that dinner party I had for a few friends at my apartment in Avalon) to call you up after you returned from your visit with your daughter in Merced and express, on the one hand, my regrets for not seeing you, and on the other, my heartfelt thanks for your eternal friendship.

After arriving in India, due to a series of unfortunate circumstances, I had to sentence myself to exile. Why did I banish myself into the limboland of self-exile? Where did I exile myself?

Let me answer these questions as truthfully as I can. To do so I must provide you with a narrative explanation with a proper sequence. I know this is extremely time-consuming, and I am anxious that this letter reach you with all possible speed. But clarity and truth are essential to give you a full picture, so that you can judge properly (and thereby show mercy) my strange midnight invasion into the privacy of your hotel room.

Readjusting to my life in Yalakki after my return from the U.S. was a Herculean and Himalayan task. I wrote several long, detailed letters to Virginia Gleason in which I clearly and minutely dissected my tortured and tormented existence. Please feel free to read those letters. I am sure that Virginia Gleason will have no objection to sharing them with you. (Perhaps they have been published in the local newspaper or even on TV and you are already familiar with them.)

She has shared them with her brother, Jeff, though it is also quite possible that those letters may have been destroyed and are gone with the wind. But if they are still alive, they will give you an honest picture of the state of my mind, body, and soul, after my return to Yalakki from Avalon.

In my two or three short letters to you, I casually mentioned my difficulties, without going into any great detail. I did this because you mentioned in one of your letters that your closest friend had passed away, that your daughter Mary was getting a divorce, and that your only sister living in San Diego was not in the best of health.

You had enough burdens. Why add more? Using that logic, I tiptoed about my troubles in my letters to you, smiling on the outside but weeping on the inside.

Unable to be patient any longer and continuing to lead what the sage of Concord, Henry David Thoreau, so aptly described as "a life of quiet desperation," I decided to listen to the voice of a different drummer and leave my wife and son and go into exile.

My initial purpose was to create a shock effect on my wife, to make her realise that the solution to my seeming madness (see my letter to Virginia Gleason for a fuller explanation of the method-in-my-madness performance) was not for her to listen to some crackpot shady astrologer but to listen to me, to abandon her obsession for material goods, and to give me her attentive ears and not her argumentative voice.

Living in my claustrophobic cubbyhole, confronted by a conceited and conniving wife, and forced to seek the relief of privacy in hysterical laughter, I realised with a growing sense of dismay that I was being pushed to the precipitous edge of insanity. I was about to become the role I was playing. The difference between me and my mask was being erased. This knowledge sent serpentine shivers of fear through my spine. Fearing for my loss of sanity, I decided to vanish.

I realised that my sudden vanishing act would bring sorrow to my old mother. Indeed, her eyes filled with tears and her hands began to tremble when I told her. But when she realised that my disappearance was temporary and that it would teach a lesson to her disobedient daughter-in-law, she readily agreed. She blessed me and urged me to disappear as soon as possible in order to achieve the transformation of her daughter-in-law.

So early one morning, around 2 A.M. to be precise, I sneaked out of the house, taking a small suitcase containing a few items to meet my basic human needs. I had absolutely no idea where I was going to begin the first chapter of my self-imposed exile.

I walked slowly, reflecting, meditating. About an hour or so later I found myself by the riverside, near the cremation grounds.

It was very quiet and peaceful except for the hoarse orchestra of some frogs. There was a gentle breeze, and I saw the flickering flames and smoke from a funeral pyre across the river. I was reminded of the mortality of man. A mood of dark melancholy hugged me like a shroud.

By the riverside was the abandoned Cobra Temple. You are familiar with this shrine, since you were brought there by my wife and her first brother. I climbed the steps to the temple and entered the spacious courtyard. I sat down, leaning against one of the four intricately carved stone pillars. The gentle breeze and the tranquil atmosphere soon coaxed and caressed me into deep slumber.

After a couple of hours I was awakened by the fartlike sounds of a bus horn. It was the early morning Yalakki to Bangalore bus. Suddenly, like a flash, I decided I would go to Bangalore and at least for a temporary period get lost in the garden city of India. I raced down the steps and ran toward the bus, which was about to leave. It was practically empty, and about four hours later I arrived in Bangalore.

Later that afternoon I ran into an American professor by the name of Henry Corbin, from Santa Barbara, California. After some chitchat over several cups of coffee and plates of cashew nuts in the India Coffee House, Corbin asked me what I was doing. "Unemployed with no immediate prospects for employment and with all the time in the world at my disposal," I replied with total honesty. He told me he was travelling around India to collect information about the lifestyle of holy men. "Not just any holy men," he explained, "but holy men who lead a dual life, a successful combination of the temporal and the spiritual. Urban holy men, as you call them here in India." He asked me if I would be willing to assist him in this project by travelling with him to the major urban and pilgrimage centers all over India. I readily agreed. He said he would take care of my food, living, and travel costs plus giving me a small stipend for incidental expenses.

Travelling with Henry Corbin and acting as his guide, companion, and interpreter proved to be one of the most rewarding experiences of my life, a heaven-sent opportunity for my discovery of India. I was able to see Madras, Bombay, Goa, Calcutta, New Delhi, Chandigarh, Benares, to mention just a few of the places. The entire travels lasted for over a year. I was able to maintain a thorough journal, recording on a daily basis my observations, experiences, and reflections. These urban holy men are just out of this world. They renounce during the day and devour all night, voraciously, if I may add. I can tell you stories that will give you perpetual gooseflesh and make your hair stand on end. I can regale you and groups of people with tales from India's urban holy land. One of these days I will write a book about these experiences, fiction or nonfiction I have not yet made up my mind. But it will be full of plots and counterplots and guaranteed to be a page turner. It has potentials for becoming a TV series far more fantastic, intriguing, and exotic than *Star Trek* that I used to watch on TV when I was in heavenly Avalon. I am sitting on a gold mine, Mrs. Neilson. No exaggeration. That is why I want you to help me. I need your help, desperately I need it, Mrs. Neilson.

Let me continue with my story to provide you with a clear picture of my present state.

It was during this year of travel that I abandoned my daily shaving habits. My beard grew thick. By constantly observing and talking to these holy men, I began unconsciously to assume some of their habits and mannerisms. I particularly watched their techniques of infinite variety and their diverse and creative strategies to win the confidence and devotion of their followers. All these techniques I have noted in my journal, and parts of it could be incorporated into a book with the catchy title, "How to Be a Holy Man: A Practical Manual." My journal is rich with encyclopedic information. "Incredible! Unbelievable!" you are bound to say when you read the several volumes of my journal. They contain material for dozens of books. No exaggeration, Mrs. Neilson, no exaggeration.

Henry Corbin was a very pleasant person to work with. He had, however, two passions: to smoke *bhang* (the leaves and flowering tips of the hemp cannabis), which is something like marijuana and to go to bed with young Punjabi boys. It was this latter passion that almost cost Henry Corbin his life in the city of Amritsar, and I had to intervene. I will refrain from telling you the details of the circumstances leading to the fight because it would be a novel in itself. It was, however, during this rescue attempt that I got my forehead slashed by a knife, and it has left a permanent scar there.

Although we sometimes had heated arguments, where I disagreed with his addiction to bhang (as for his passion for pubescent boys, my attitude was one of gentle tolerance, live and let live), we had become attached, Henry Corbin and myself. So when the time came for him to fly back to California, parting did indeed become such sweet sorrow!

Henry Corbin had been impressed with my help. I shared with him my desire to return to America. He suggested that I get in touch with a group called "The One and Only," headquartered in Los Angeles. I believe this group is very much devoted to learning about Eastern cults. Henry Corbin said that he would explore possibilities with them for an invitation to be extended to me for returning to the U.S. to deliver a series of lectures. But I have not heard from Henry Corbin. I do not have his address to write and remind him, because at the time he left he had no permanent address. Also, he was not planning to be in California for very long but was taking off for parts of North Africa to continue his research into urban holy men in that part of the world. He had already lined up a Moroccan student from UCLA to serve as his guide.

Mrs. Neilson, I would very much like to request you to kindly check out for me the group called "The One and Only." Their address is 201 Yucca Street, Los Angeles. More on that later.

Let me continue my narration.

Henry Corbin flew home from Calcutta, and I "hung out" (I love that American phrase) in Calcutta for a few days. I grew homesick for Yalakki, for my mother, for my wife's cooking, and even for my wife's company. Absence makes the heart grow fonder!

I decided to return to Yalakki. It took me nearly a month to reach Bangalore because I travelled the entire distance without buying a ticket. It is one of the benefits I derived from studying the lives of urban holy men. They are past masters in the art of ticketless travel.

This return-ticketless-train-travel trip all across this vast and ancient land, more specifically from Calcutta to Bangalore, could also be written up for publication. "The Trials and Tribulations of a Ticketless Traveler: A Self-Confession" would again be a catchy title. I have kept elaborate notes of this travel. But more on that later.

So you see, Mrs. Neilson, by getting lost, I discovered myself and my country. I wish to disseminate my knowledge, both for purposes of spreading culture as well as earning some hard cash. Your help in achieving these twin purposes is of paramount importance.

But to continue. I took the last bus from Bangalore to Yalakki. My perfect record of blemishless, ticketless travel was spoiled because of the stubborn bus driver. I was compelled to buy a ticket.

The reason I am giving you all this minute information, Mrs. Neilson, is to demonstrate my sincere desire to be perfectly honest with you. I am telling you the whole truth and nothing but the truth. I will hide nothing from you, including my letters to V. Gleason and whatever I might have stated there in the heat of passion.

There were only four passengers on that bus from Bangalore to Yalakki. No one recognised me. I arrived in Yalakki a little after midnight. When I asked the driver to let me off at the three-rock stop, he asked: "Three-rock stop? Are you not afraid of getting off there at this time of night?" "You have nothing to fear but fear itself," I replied with serenity, borrowing, of course, the words from one of your own distinguished former presidents.

The night was suffocatingly hot when I got off the bus. There was no wind. I walked towards the abandoned Cobra Temple, stripped to my loincloth, and bathed in the river. Then I dried myself and entered the temple courtyard and sat down. I ate two bananas and some groundnuts (peanuts as you call them) which I had bought near the Bangalore bus stand. Then I spread a sheet on the floor and went to sleep.

It was my intention to get up early in the morning and establish contact with my mother. I was confident that my mother would inform me that my exile had achieved its purpose by transforming my wife from an aggressive person to a more submissive one. I was equally confident that my mother, with her years of common sense, would help me plot my reappearance in the house. I also looked forward to a big, fresh cup of strong Mysore coffee, for which my mother is famous. My wife too for that matter.

But in the early hours of the morning as the cool breeze from the river woke me up, I was thinking of getting up when I heard some people enter the temple courtyard. They were conversing. I immediately recognised one voice. It was the unmistakable, shrill voice of my wife. Ah, she has found out, I thought, and tensed up as I assumed a fetal position, preparing myself for her merciless onslaught: "I know, I know. You are there beneath that sheet. Do you think you could hide from me?"

To confess or not to confess, that was the dilemma I faced. Should I calmly rise and say with a tranquil mind and a serene heart: "Yes, I am here. But I am not the same person you think I am. I have renounced worldly life. I have solemnly taken the vows of a *sanyasi*. I have just returned from Benares, where, under the inspired blessings of a guru, I entered *samadhi*. I am here to see my mother, touch her feet, get her blessings. I am here to see my son, bless him. Then I leave."

While I framed these words, I heard the constantly clearing, hoarse-throated voice of the other person. It definitely belonged to that conniving astrologer. Could he have located me? Did he really have such powers? I wondered.

He started to counsel my wife. "Let us sit and talk. Unless you have complete faith and trust in my powers, nothing can be achieved. So, Vimalamma, please be patient."

He was addressing my wife with such respect! It was a real snow job. But I breathed a sigh of relief. Truth was not out, yet. My secret was safe!

They were up to something, my wife and that good-for-nothing astrologer. Destiny, I realized, had placed me in a unique position, providing me with a ringside seat (so to speak) to listen to a diabolical plot being hatched, yes, definitely diabolical.

Either the sari of my wife or the dhoti of the astrologer brushed my body as they walked by me, a further sign that they ignored me completely, thinking that the body beneath the sheet belonged to some starving beggar. I thanked the fates for my good fortune. I heard them sit not too far from me and begin to talk. I will try to recollect their dialogue to the best of my ability.

MY WIFE: First you must be honest with me. I am betrayed by everyone. That is my fate. I trust people. People don't show trust to me. They tell lies, take advantage of my soft nature. Do you know how difficult it was to get you that money? Then you take it and suddenly disappear. Just like my husband.

ASTROLOGER: Vimalamma, please listen. I did not disappear. Have I done something shameful that I must disappear like your husband? I had to go out of Yalakki because of pressure of work. What can I do? Do you know the Zamindar of Kanathur? Never mind if you don't. His youngest son was missing, so I was summoned to help. Can I refuse the cry for help from a father in sorrow? His family have been my clients for many, many years. So I went to Kanathur as fast as I could. In fact, before I left, I asked Ramu. . . .

MY WIFE: Ramu? Which Ramu?

ASTROLOGER: Ramu, that orphan boy who begs in front of Bhatta's Neo-Café. Did he not tell you?

MY WIFE: No Ramu, no Geemu. (Mrs. Neilson, remember my telling you how we Indians like to make instant word rhymes while we talk. My wife may be the best—or worst—at it in the whole subcontinent.)

ASTROLOGER: That scoundrel. I gave him some money and told him to run to your house and deliver the message. Who can you trust these days? Who, I ask you?

MY WIFE: No one. Absolutely no one.

ASTROLOGER: You are absolutely right, Vimalamma, you cannot trust anyone these days.

MY WIFE: I agree. So did you find the Zamindar's missing son?

ASTROLOGER: Yes. Just as I had prophesied. In the exact place, at the exact spot, at the exact time I had said they would find him, the Zamindar found his son. They were overjoyed. I was too. But for nearly ten days after the boy was found, I

94

was unable to think or sleep because of severe headache. Severe.

MY WIFE: Why severe headache?

ASTROLOGER: Because of concentration, Vimalamma. Concentration. The entire powers of the body and mind must be fused to remove the veils and penetrate the darkness to see where the boy was. Lots of mental power must be used. That is very exhausting. It is equivalent to carrying hundreds and thousands of tons of heavy materials on your back for twenty minutes. Intense, very intense.

MY WIFE: Why don't you use those powers and tell me where my husband is?

ASTROLOGER: I have told you where your husband is. He is in another part of the world.

MY WIFE: That is correct. But that woman to whom I wrote, Virginia Gleason, the secret paramour of my husband, says that he is not there.

ASTROLOGER: Will she tell you the truth? She is his paramour. Do you expect her to tell you the truth?

MY WIFE: No.

ASTROLOGER: So you see! I am right.

MY WIFE: You are right, I am right. But what to do to solve my problem?

ASTROLOGER: You have to do what I have been telling you to do, Vimalamma. If you want your husband to return to you, particularly with his money, which is rightfully yours, then you must do all that is necessary to achieve that purpose. Delay is dangerous. Speed is success. The sooner we begin to perform the various ceremonies, the better it is.

MY WIFE: Money, money, money. It is always money. But where to get it? Where? You tell me. Where to get five thousand rupees for all the ceremonies? Where? (Five thousand rupees! My ears widened at the mention of that figure. That astrologer was indeed aiming high.)

ASTROLOGER: Let me again explain the reason for these ceremonies. They will be performed in Bellary by a very reputed person. As a matter of fact it will be under the personal supervision of my former teacher. The ceremonies will influence your husband to return to India, to Yalakki, to you, and to your son. Your husband has accumulated a considerable amount of money in America. All that is yours. Because of the hardship your husband has put you through, that money belongs to you. It will come to you, I assure you, once the ceremonies are performed. What is five thousand compared to lifelong prosperity?

My Wife: I know, I know. But how to get it? Where to get it?

Astrologer: You have those American dollars. . . .

My Wife: (Quickly interrupting him. Shock in her voice.) How do you know about my American dollars?

Astrologer: How can you ask such a question? Knowing hidden things is my business. Why do you want my service? My help? Why? Have I not seen across oceans and land and told you where your husband is? Have I not?

I felt like jumping up and confronting him and screaming: "You fool, you bogus stargazer. I am here, right here, not across the oceans." But I restrained myself and held my tongue.

Mrs. Neilson, for the sake of brevity, let me summarise the rest of their repulsive conversation. They cooked up a plot. Actually he cooked it, she stirred the plot pot. He wanted some more money to perform some long-distance black magic on Virginia Gleason. That magic was expected to turn Gleason into a law-abiding American citizen and make her report me to the Immigration Service so that I would be deported. He was dishing out unadulterated nonsense, and my wife was swallowing it.

I had hoped that because of my wife's association with me and because of my having provided her that golden opportunity to visit America (with your generous help), she would not be that stupid to believe the blatant lies and hogwash that the good-for-nothing astrologer was feeding her. But money or the promise of money makes people lose their sense of reason. Gold has always been my wife's god.

The astrologer was fully aware of this weakness of my wife, her passion for money and material possessions. So he applied all his pressure on that weak spot. He therefore resumed his sales pitch with unabated vigor.

I became curious about the American dollars my wife had. I had certainly not given her any. I wondered if she had written to you, begging for help, and whether you, with your usual generosity, had sent her some money.

The mystery soon cleared up when my wife told the astrologer how she had come by those American dollars. "I am amazed how you have found out about my American dollars," my wife began. "No one knows about it. I taught some American ladies how to prepare Indian food. Also I carried on a small side business by selling some lemon pickles, etc. The money I got from these activities I saved. But it is really very surprising that you have come to know about my American dollars. All I have is one hundred and twenty-five dollars. Certainly that will not come to five thousand rupees."

"Do not worry," the astrologer said. "I have private connections where you can get black market prices."

Black market, black magic, that satanic astrologer was into everything devious and criminal. He was also a trained salesman, and so he made his final pitch. "Vimalamma," he began, "it is your decision whether to spend the money or not. But you have to make a quick decision. I cannot wait forever. There is too much evil in the world. Therefore, there is too much demand for my help. I have other matters to attend to. So all I am saying is that by this evening you must tell me, yes or no. I can also get you a good price for your house from that Shetty whom I have helped in many transactions. So from the sale of the house you can easily raise five thousand rupees. But it is your decision. I have to go."

He left.

He was after my cubbyhole house too. Greedy goat!

I felt sad for my stupid wife, sad that she could be duped so easily. I wondered if I should rise and put a stop to all this, expose myself and expose the astrologer as well.

I heard my wife sigh and get up. Then she left.

I lay there for a few more minutes and then sat up. Mrs. Neilson, I was confused, perplexed, puzzled. I yearned for a cup of steaming coffee. I yearned for a nice hot bath as well.

97

I folded the sheet and put it into my battered suitcase, took out a towel, and walked down the steps to the river to bathe and collect my thoughts. I was about to walk back to the shore to dry myself and go to a restaurant when I saw my wife. She was about three hundred feet away from me. She looked very thoughtful and was slowly walking toward me with her head bowed. She was dabbing her eyes with the flap end of her sari. Was she crying? I wondered.

I quickly turned away and sat down by the edge of the river, submerged up to my waist in water. I reached for my dark glasses, which I had left on a towel by the edge of the river, covered my eyes, and pretended to meditate.

As my wife walked close by, she noticed me. She paused, folded her hands in front of her and bowed to me, performing the automatic gesture of most Indians when they see a person of religious aura. Another proof that she had not recognised me.

I took the risk and uttered one of those universally applicable statements that *sadhus* make to people to catch their attention. "Have faith. All your troubles will soon be over," I said in a very gentle voice.

With a surprise and sparkle in her voice she asked, "How did you know I have troubles? You are so right. So absolutely right. I have troubles. A sea of troubles."

She moved close to me.

I waved my hand, asking her to keep her distance.

"Yes, yes," she said and retreated.

I again gestured with my hand, suggesting she sit down.

She obeyed. "Do you really think . . ." she started.

I raised my palm suggesting that she keep silent.

She obeyed.

I looked away from her and gazed across the river. I was now firmly convinced that she had definitely not recognised me. Was it the thick, luxuriant beard? Was it the dark glasses? Was it the scar on my forehead? Was it the extra weight I had gained? Or was it the firm belief planted in her mind by that crooked astrologer that I was in America under the influence of Virginia Gleason? Maybe a combination of all these factors. But my wife had not recognised me.

After sufficient pause to lend weight to my words, I said with dramatic pauses between each and every word: "You are thinking of your husband. He is also thinking of you. He is not here, not in this country. He is in a land beyond the oceans."

"True, true. Very true," she interjected quickly.

I raised my palm, suggesting she control her enthusiasm.

She obeyed.

In a well-modulated voice suited to the role of a sadhu, I spoke slowly and clearly, making just enough references to my wife's past life both in India and in America to convince her that I possessed the powers to unveil the past and peer into the future. She is such a simpleton. She believed me. She became ecstatic in her praise of my powers. She was ready to prostrate herself at my feet and declare lifelong obedience.

I discouraged her from such effusive demonstrations. I got up and said, "Do not trust false astrologers. Have faith in God," and quickly waded into the river and started to bathe and immerse myself in the waters. When I emerged she was gone.

I felt both elated and frightened at the coup I had pulled off. It had happened so fast, so smoothly, and so convincingly.

The frightening part was how to keep it up. How would I get out of it? *What* would I get out of it! Well, answers will reveal themselves to me, I consoled myself. I would play it by ear, I decided.

I returned to the shore, dried myself, and, dressed only in a loin-cloth, walked back to the temple courtyard. The sun had come up in all his blazing glory. It was going to be another hot day.

I surveyed the courtyard. At least in the immediately foreseeable future this abandoned Cobra Temple, this place with its aura of black magic and witchcraft, this stone structure with its dark echoes of curses and conspiracies, was going to be my headquarters. I realised that no sadhu had staked his claim to this abandoned Cobra Temple. No one had been courageous enough to do that.

An urban holy man I had come across in the city of Allahabad had been eminently successful because he had staked out an abandoned temple, a temple that reeked with notoriety as a center for plotting evil. The fact that he had challenged such evil forces and rehabilitated the temple had increased his strength, his credibility, and his charisma in the eyes of his devotees, who had spread the word and brought in more devotees.

I decided to do the same for this abandoned Cobra Temple in my hometown of Yalakki. My wife's faith in me would increase. I could wean her away from the influence of that cutthroat lawyer-turned-astrologer. As a lawyer he had ruined families through long, tangled litigations. Now he was ruining people through planetary premonitions about which he knew nothing.

I finally concluded that my getting off at three-rock stop, spending the night in the courtyard of the abandoned Cobra Temple, overhearing the conversation between my wife and the bogus astrologer, and subsequently impressing my wife were all part of a plan, perhaps a divine plan. I decided to perform my present role with faith and conviction. I was going to give it all I had. That's what you used to tell me, Mrs. Neilson: "Raj, give it all you've got!"

There was the courtyard with its intricately carved stone pillars. In the center of these pillars was the impressive marble sculpture of the black, coiled, hooded cobra. In front of this sculpture was the inner sanctuary of the temple. The door to the sanctuary was closed. It had been closed for as long as I could remember.

If I had to stay here, and I had decided to do so, I had to open the door to this inner sanctuary, enter, survey, and make it habitable for my abode. Thus I reasoned.

The sun was bright. The place was quiet. I murmured a prayer, took a deep breath, and opened the wooded door with brass knobs and strips. I had expected the door to be stuck, but it yielded easily and opened into the sanctuary.

The sanctuary was empty. Just empty. A hollow emptiness. Another surprise. I had expected the place to be full of cobwebs, broken bricks, peeling walls, musty smell, and gothic echoes, but it was clean. The stone walls were bare. The stone floor was equally bare but covered with a thin film of dust. From the ceiling hung a brass bell with its tongue missing. There were three grill windows above the front wall facing me. In the right-hand corner of the room was a tap. I turned it, and after a gurgle and a gutter, water stuttered out.

Perfect, I thought. I would sweep it and light some sandalwood sticks to help remove the musty odor. I would remove the three bars on each of the windows for more air and light. I could easily get a rope cot and other basic essentials. The indoor tap was an added convenience. The hinges of the door needed a little oil.

Yes. It would do for my sanctuary, I concluded.

I was certain that my wife would return. I was positive that word would spread and bring in a few more devotees. They would bring food, fruits, milk, and even some loose change as offerings. Beggar boys would trickle in to begin their begging and thereby provide an outlet for the charity of the devotees. One or two of the beggar boys would not only beg but start their own business by offering to watch over the footwear of the devotees for a small fee. Vendors would set up their stalls and sell flowers, bananas, coconuts, camphor, etc., etc. Thus, my rehabilitating the abandoned Cobra Temple would generate minor industries connected with this holy man business. It would provide some small employment to a few more people. That was a comforting thought.

I would select a beggar boy to take care of my needs. He would guard the door of my sanctuary and thereby ensure my privacy. He would instruct my devotees to stand in line and take their turn as they trooped in to get my *darshan* (a form of unique joy, a sense of glow that devotees get by being in the presence of a great person, a great place, or even a great thing). He would also announce the times when I would grant darshana to the devotees. He would report to me on · matters I wanted reported on. He would be my eyes and ears when I rested within my sanctuary.

Perfect, I thought again, as I planned my holy man's role, marvelling at the way things had happened and were going to happen.

I felt the pangs of hunger and wished that my wife would soon return with food and fruits, and I hoped she would bring a hot cup of coffee as well.

Perseverance is the hinge of all virtues, so I waited patiently, even as the inner man growled with hunger.

About three or four hours later, I heard the voices of some people approaching the temple. I quickly returned to my sanctuary and left the door slightly ajar.

I heard my wife's voice and . . . horrors, that of her first brother as well.

"Swamiji, Swamiji," she called out. "Please take some food. Some fruits," she added.

I did not reply immediately.

"Swamiji, please take some food, some fruits. Please." It was her first brother making his request.

"Please leave the food and depart. Do not disturb me now," I replied as solemnly as I could.

"Swamiji, does my brother-in-law really have a lot of money in America?" It was her first brother, greedy as ever for money.

"Come tomorrow morning," I said in a very commanding voice and pushed the door shut with my foot.

I heard them whisper to each other for a minute or two and then leave.

I emerged from my sanctuary. The food and fruits were a welcome sight. My mouth watered. I ate heartily. The mangoes were sweet and succulent. My wife's cooking was as good as ever. The only thing missing was a good hot cup of coffee. The milk was lukewarm, but I drank it anyway.

So, Mrs. Neilson, this is how I got into my holy man, sadhu, swamiji role. Advertently? Inadvertently? Who can say. Did it begin when I met Henry Corbin and agreed to assist him in his project about urban holy men? Or did it begin when my wife bowed to me and thereby confirmed my disguised identity as genuine, by mistaking the mask for the man? Whatever, enough of such speculation.

I have now been a sadhu for nearly seven to eight months. Frankly, I had not expected it to last this long. Somehow I thought that I would be able to extricate myself from this self-created trap (for it has become a trap—why mince words?) within a short period.

Mrs. Neilson, I am sure that during your brief visit to my sanctuary, you noticed how the crowds were attracted to me, like flies to sweets. I am both amazed and disturbed by this crowded congregation continuously increasing day by day, sometimes even hour by hour. I have worked no miracles to receive such adulation. I have not declared that I am a miracle worker. For my wife, yes, I have done a few things that have the aura of a miracle. A few times I have surreptitiously sneaked out and deposited small amounts of money in certain unlikely places. Then I have directed my wife to these places. A sort of treasure hunt with specific instructions as to where the treasure is! I was motivated by three reasons to do such bogus miracles. First, the desire to lure my wife away from the clutches of that illegal astrologer who had plotted to take everything she had, including my cubbyhole house. Second, to make my wife have faith in me. Is there any surer way to win the faith of a materialistic person than to increase his material wealth? Third, by a genuine desire to help my wife and son meet some of their daily needs.

As for the crowded congregation, I have done nothing to improve their condition, materially or spiritually, either collectively or individually. I merely listen to each and every one as they come to see me. I bless them and drop a flower into their open palms, a flower they themselves have brought as an offering to me.

During my travels with Henry Corbin I discovered that most people who visit sadhus do not question their powers. They do not talk out against the sadhu. This is particularly true in small towns like Yalakki. If a devotee does not find what he is looking for, he will quietly stop coming and blame his karma for lack of success, and never the sadhu. The sadhu often represents the powers of the unknown, and the unknown is always full of fear for the simple devotee. The mystique of power, of an ability to curse and bring evil, surrounds the sadhu. Who would want to risk the wrath of such supernatural powers by expressing doubts about him? Besides, miracles are usually the result of intense faith, unquestioning acceptance, and that requires time—long periods of time. The sadhu can always answer skeptics with this reason.

My travels with Henry Corbin have given me an out—my beggar-boy-turned-guardian Subbu, whom I nurtured from an all-bones-and-eyes skinny boy to a plump butterball and who has been serving as the guardian of my sanctuary door.

Subbu is the one who came and whispered to me: "There is a foreign white woman with Vimalamma. How tall she is! As tall as the coconut tree outside." Immediately I knew it was you. Should I come out or not come out? I wrestled with the dilemma and then instructed Subbu to go and announce: "Swamiji is cancelling darshan for today!"

Subbu, unfortunately, is not to be trusted. Outwardly he calls me "Swamiji, Swamiji" with sugar-sweetened syllables, and touches my feet reverentially. But he knows I am bogus, counterfeit, with feet of clay and the passions of mortal men. He knows of my addiction to coffee and cigarettes. He has supplied these to me. Of course I pay for them, plus some tips to keep his mouth shut. One time he even asked me with a sly grin whether I wanted the companionship of a girl and started to describe her attributes. I stared at him so hard he hung down his head, asked my apology, and touched my feet.

The very fact that Subbu asked such a question is a clear sign that he must have noticed the flames of desire in my eyes. It is a warning to me to be cautious.

I am also troubled with doubts concerning my wife, even though I do not have any concrete evidence to indicate that she might have recognised me for what I am, namely, her husband. She continues to behave with extreme respect, courtesy, and humility. In fact a bit too much respect, if I may say so. She faithfully informed me of your letter announcing your intended trip to Yalakki, thereby complying with my earlier instructions to her asking her to keep me closely informed of any letter or communication her husband might receive from overseas. She also told me that she followed my instructions and sent you a cable asking you not to come.

Mrs. Neilson, my question to you is: Did my wife send you a cable? I must know the answer to this crucial question. Please, tell me the truth. In your thank-you-for-your-hospitality letter that you will be writing to my wife, you can include the word *cable* somehow or other. If the word *cable* is included, then I will know that my wife is telling the truth. If the word is omitted, then I will know that she is lying.

I asked my wife: "Why did the American woman, the friend of your husband, show up in Yalakki? Did you not send her the cable?"

Her reply was: "What can I do? I sent the cable. But she still decided to come. She insisted on seeing you. Americans are crazy about holy men."

My wife told me how a thief had broken into your hotel room and asked me for my opinion. "Who do you think would have perpetrated such a crime? Swamiji, you know the answer. Can you please tell me?"

I replied: "There was no break-in. No thief entered the hotel room of the American woman. It was her intense imagination, her desire for some kind of excitement, her desire to have a story which she could narrate to her friends in America that made her imagine a thief had broken into her room. Sometimes imagination is so intense that it becomes reality."

My wife nodded her head.

I am still suspicious that she knows. She may nod and nod and yet, Mrs. Neilson, when I was in Tirupathi with Henry Corbin, a young boy from Yalakki by the name of Sheshu recognized me. Sheshu's mother (now dead) and my wife were very close friends. Did Sheshu return to Yalakki and tell my wife that he had seen me? I am now suddenly plagued by all these doubts.

Returning to Subbu. He knows of my entry into your hotel room. He was to warn me if anyone approached the area outside your room.

Subbu has enough ammunition to explode me, to blow me to kingdom come if he wants to.

Crowds continue to increase. I am totally boxed in. I have no privacy at all. Every move of mine is being watched. Even the few hours of solitude I had between midnight and four A.M. when I could emerge from my sanctuary and smoke and reflect have been taken away from me.

I have become the prisoner of my own plot.

People, people, everywhere (if Samuel Taylor Coleridge will pardon me paraphrasing his immortal words). Not a moment for myself.

I wish I were an urban holy man, spiritual by day and swinger by night.

I overheard my wife's brother telling Subbu that he was planning to get a reporter from Bangalore's *Deccan Herald* to visit Yalakki and come to my sanctuary to write a story about me. That's all I need! You know how newspaper reporters are. Bloodhounds! I must avoid that at all costs.

Time is of the essence. There is no time to lose. I could cancel all darshanas. I could say I have entered into the state of deep samadhi. But these can only be temporary measures, just to buy time.

So you see the fix I am in. You can appreciate the mess. It is this fix, this being-sucked-into-quicksand situation that compelled me to take the drastic, high-risk step to see you. I wanted to tell you face-to-face these facts I have now written. This is the honest reason for my break-in.

But my mission failed miserably.

Mrs. Neilson, I must return to America. I have been telling my wife that her husband will send for her and her son from there.

Please, Mrs. Neilson, contact The One and Only group. Urge them to be my sponsors. Their official letter of invitation and sponsorship can be addressed to: Swamiji of Yalakki, care of my wife's address. She will bring it to me.

Once I reach America, I can go on a nationwide lecture tour and speak about sadhus, swamis, and gurus from an insider's point of view. I will devote myself to writing fiction and nonfiction, TV and movie scripts—all based on my rich and diverse experiences as a holy man.

Please help me, Mrs. Neilson. I know you can, if you make up your mind. I will be eternally grateful to you. I have told you the entire truth, my strengths and my weaknesses.

I hope you can make out my handwriting. It is a windy night and the light from the kerosene lamp is flickering. The pressure to finish this letter and send it on its way to you is unbearable. Even if some of the words are illegible, I am sure you can hear the cry of anguish and the plea for help that screams out from these pages.

Please be assured that I will reimburse whatever expenses are involved in helping me to return to America.

I am sitting on a gold mine, Mrs. Neilson, a veritable gold mine. That is no exaggeration.

> Thank you for helping me. I know you will.
> Your friend, no, more than that, your son,
> Raj

Wow! I said to myself after finishing the letter. That's our Raj! I took a break, walked around the block, returned, and picked up Vimala's long epistle.

3

My dearest Mrs. Neilson:

This letter, I am finally writing.

First, I wrote a very short and sweet letter. In it I said that I was saddened not to see you before you returned to America. I wrote, have a safe and sound trip to your homeland, and ended my letter.

When I took this short letter to the post office, I got some very shocking information. Because of that information I decided not to post the short and sweet letter. On my way home I decided to write and tell you the complete story.

I have spent nearly five days to write this letter. I remembered your advice when I was in Avalon. You were always telling me, Vimala, use simple words and simple sentences, just like in the Bible. Well, Mrs. Neilson, I have done my best to follow that advice. But I am writing about a very complicated matter. So please forgive my many mistakes and for any long sentences I may have made.

Man proposes. But God disposes. How very true.

As you know, on Wednesday night after returning from the deserted Cobra Temple, we had made plans to meet at the Modern Hotel on Thursday morning at seven and enjoy breakfast together. Then Kittu, my first brother, and myself wished very much to take you to the parrot bird sanctuary. After that we were going to take you to the railway station so that you could take the train to Bangalore.

But man proposes. God disposes.

The three of us, Kittu, myself, and my first brother, arrived at the hotel on Thursday morning. Unfortunately, we arrived two hours late. My brother's car would not start. He had loaned it to a so-called friend of his. This friend had mishandled it. At least this friend should have told my brother about the damaged car. Instead, he simply pushed the car in front of my brother's house and left. It was only in the morning that my brother realised something was wrong with the car. He tried his best to start it, but the car was totally damaged. My brother has decided to take my advice from now on and not lend the car to unreliable fair-weather friends. But that is like locking the house after the thief has stolen the silver dishes.

Thursday morning I got up very early and prepared some hot *idlis*

and mildly spiced onion *sambhar*, plus fresh ghee to bring to you. I
wanted you to have a sample taste of simple home-cooked food. Actually, we should have invited you for a good dinner, served South
Indian style on a fresh green banana leaf. But your visit was brief.
There was not sufficient time to prepare the simple but affectionate
feast in the proper manner. So please forgive me.

When my brother's car would not start, Kittu ran over to the
taxi stand and managed to bring one. But the fates were against us.
They were determined to see that we should not meet. The main road
leading to the hotel was fully occupied by a funeral procession. All
the honking, horning, and shouting by the driver was unable to clear
the path. So we had to take a long, roundabout road to reach the
hotel.

This is the reason for the delay in arriving at the hotel. Now you
know. When we arrived at the hotel we found out that you had
already left. When I heard about what had happened to you the night
before, I simply collapsed. This is a thorough disgrace to all of us, to
all of India in fact.

We wanted immediately to rush over to the railway station. I
determined right then to tell you the truth about my husband. But the
taxi had left. My brother should not have paid the taxi driver so soon.
But he had. So we had to send Kittu to get an auto rickshaw. This
consumed more time. When the auto rickshaw arrived, the driver
refused to take three people in it. He categorized my son Kittu as an
adult and not as a child. Kittu looks tall, but he is just a child, I
argued. But the auto rickshaw fellow would not agree.

Finally my brother decided to stay, and Kittu and I took the auto
rickshaw to the railway station. But due to our bad luck, fates were
once again against us. The train had left punctually on time! Kittu
tried to console me. Then he too started to weep, remembering your
kindness and how you had brought him a gift of chocolates all the way
from America. Please accept our heartfelt apologies, mine and Kittu's.
We are very sorry for what happened to you. Let not this ugly incident
give you a bad impression of Yalakki, of India, and of us.

Now, Mrs. Neilson, I must tell you some very unpleasant facts.
It is not easy to do this. But in the interests of truth, I must. I have
no other choice.

The thief who broke into your hotel room is my husband. Does this shock you, Mrs. Neilson? Are you even now as you read this sentence saying, with your mouth open, What? It is the truth, Mrs. Neilson. Truth is shocking.

As you know, my husband disappeared one morning, nearly a year ago. What you don't know is that he had been behaving very strangely ever since he arrived from America. Each and every time I wanted to talk with him, he would go to his room and lock the door. He would start typing. Typing what? God only knows.

After some weeks he gave up typing and began to laugh. Just laugh for no reason. Everyone thought he was mad. Who is to blame for his madness? Naturally the finger was pointed at me. My mother-in-law headed the list, others imitated her.

As you know, I am a very patient person. I like peace all the time. Do you remember how you asked me to go for a ride with you one morning in Avalon? I agreed. Then you told me that my husband was having difficulties concentrating on his studies. Do you remember how I quickly asked you, Is it because of me, Mrs. Neilson? Do you remember how you coughed and hesitated to reply? Do you remember how I said, Mrs. Neilson, my husband's happiness is my happiness. I will return to Yalakki with my son Kittu, let my husband fully concentrate on his studies, get his degree, and return with honor. Did I make any fuss? You know I did not. I say this only as an example of my peaceful nature. I will give trouble to myself, but to others I will not give trouble. That is my simple but sincere philosophy.

So when everyone began to accuse me and say that because of me, my husband has become mad, I simply accepted it with patience and humility. I knew in my heart of heart that my husband was not mad. He was pretending to use madness as an excuse to leave me.

He has never liked me. That is a fact, Mrs. Neilson. He is in love with a woman called Saroja. He wanted me to be a duplicate of this woman. When he wrote letters to me from Avalon, he told me how to prepare myself for arrival in America. Every letter contained orders from him asking me to observe Saroja and imitate her dress and her style. Saroja is the only daughter of a rich man who has married the only son of another rich man. Me, I am the fifth daughter of a retired primary school teacher, married to the third son of a retired water inspector.

With what Saroja spends one day on her powders and perfumes and Ponds cream and her special hair oils, we could have enough food for one complete month. How can I imitate her? Why should I imitate her? I have my own natural beauty. That is enough for me. Why should I cover up my natural beauty with Saroja's artificial beauty? Her face is full of pockmarks, all carefully covered up with thick layers of Ponds cream, dusted over by Kashmir Fragrance talcum powder. I know this because I have seen her very closely. My husband has seen her from a distance, and from a distance anything looks beautiful, even a stone- and shrub-covered mountain. My husband thinks that Saroja is like a beautiful film star, the Indian version of Marilyn Monroe.

From the very beginning, my mother-in-law has been against our marriage. But because of her daughter, she had to agree. I will now tell you how our marriage took place. I want to be completely honest with you.

Shuba, my husband's youngest sister, had reached marriageable age. The entire family was having a difficult time finding her a husband. Shuba is not good-looking. She is not well educated. Added to this she has a very short temper. Total, three disqualifications. But my mother-in-law and company wanted to give her a whitewash and get her married off to some innocent boy. A very difficult task, I must say. Can an ordinary stone be made into a diamond? Can a crow sing like a nightingale?

They heard about an available bridegroom in Kolar, my town. My father knew this bridegroom very well because he had been a student of my father. The bridegroom was also an orphan and therefore he often ate and slept in our house. So when my future husband and his elder brother arrived in Kolar in search of a bridegroom, they came to our house to ask my father to use his influence and persuade the orphan bridegroom to marry Shuba. My father, who was a very generous saintlike person, was ready to help. My mother, who is not so saintlike but more clever, told my father that he should get a favor in return for his help. What favor? my father asked. To get Vimala married, my mother replied. Tell them, my mother told my father, that you will persuade the orphan bridegroom to marry Shuba, if my future husband would marry me. My father hesitated. My mother insisted. Discussion, arguments, negotiations, consultations, etc. followed. Finally, agreement was reached. So Shuba got married to the orphan bridegroom and I got married to my future husband who became my present husband. As you Americans say, my marriage was a trade-off.

The orphan bridegroom's name is Lakshmi Narayana Venkateshwara Sharma. Because it is so long, I am in one way Americanising his name to orphan bridegroom. I want to tell you everything, Mrs. Neilson. I will not hide anything from you, however small it is.

Several times my husband has told me to my face, I only married you to help my sister. In spite of this, his sister Shuba hates me. If it were not for me, she would never have gotten a husband without laying down a big dowry. The orphan bridegroom was a simple person before he got married. After he married Shuba, he has become awful. She has totally robbed him of his simple innocence. Because of her demands for new saris, her constant desire to eat in restaurants and go to movies, the orphan bridegroom began to take bribes. It was found out, the poor boy lost his job and respect. Job you can get again, but respect, never.

Anyway, one morning my husband disappeared. He wanted to shock me. Why? God only knows. When he did not return after six or seven weeks, I became very worried. Meanwhile my mother-in-law started her abuses of me. The tug-of-war between her and me is not new. She has never liked me because I did not bring any dowry for her son. But I brought her a son-in-law. That she has forgotten. My father could never afford a dowry. I would have opposed it anyway. Dowry system is a dirty business. It is very humiliating to the bride. Lots of tragedies have taken place because of this dowry business. One of my best friends, Shanta, committed suicide because of this dirty dowry business. Her father had been unable to pay up the balance of her dowry after the wedding. Her mother-in-law persuaded her son to send Shanta back to her parents and stay there until the dowry balance was settled. Shanta's husband obeyed his mother. Most Indian husbands are controlled by their mothers. Shanta left, but on the way to her parents' house, she jumped into a well and took her life. Later it was discovered that she was two months pregnant.

I asked my mother-in-law if she knew where my husband was. No need to tell me where he is, just tell me he is safe, I said. All I got in reply was either loud sobbing or nonstop accusations. Out of respect for her age I kept quiet. Although she has two other sons and three daughters, she continues to stay with us. That is because none of her other children will have her.

After my husband disappeared, my mother-in-law invited all her sons and daughters to arrive with their families. I knew she was preparing for a big war to push me out of the house. So I sent for my second brother to come. Unfortunately, he could not. I think he must have come under the influence of his wife who must have told him, Do not get involved in other people's affairs. Marriage changes people overnight. My first brother, who has always supported me, had to be out of town. Therefore, when all my in-laws arrived, there was no one to take my side. I was alone with my son Kittu. They were terrible days, terrible. The very remembrance brings rivers of tears to my eyes.

I tried hard to find out where my husband was. I wrote to Miss Virginia Gleason in Avalon. She and my husband were always writing letters to each other. She once wrote to him saying that if he did not like it in India, he should return to America. Miss Gleason replied to me saying that she did not know where my husband was.

I very much wanted to write to you, but you had written on your Christmas card that you were moving to San Diego to live with your sister. I did not have the San Diego address. Also I did not want to trouble you.

My life became miserable. My mother-in-law spread rumors and gossip about me. Poor Kittu did not know what to believe. Even he asked me once if I had sent his father away because of my loud mouth. My heart was ready to burst.

One night I became so depressed and disgusted that to seek some peace of mind, I went to Lord Genesha Temple and sat on the stone steps. During the day the temple is crowded with people, mostly students who come to pray. But at nighttime there is no one and it is very peaceful and quiet. While I was sitting and seriously thinking about my life, a young man entered the temple. He asked me what I was doing there at that time of the night. I recognised him. It was

Sheshu. His mother wrote to me when I was in Avalon asking me if I could send her son a copy of Gray's *Anatomy* book.

You will remember, Mrs. Neilson, I called you on the phone and requested you to help me by sending a copy of Gray's *Anatomy* book to Sheshu. Then in one week or less, you were able to secure for me a copy of Gray's *Anatomy* from one of your nephews attending medical school in Minnesota. You even paid for the postage, airmail, to send it to Sheshu. You may also remember that you received a thank-you letter from Sheshu for your generous lifelong gift, along with a sandal-wood paper cutter as a token of his appreciation.

Sheshu is now attending medical college in Vellore. But when I saw him he was visiting Yalakki and had come to the Ganesha Temple to offer his prayers.

I think I know why you are sitting here, very sad and full of thoughts, Sheshu said to me. You have been helpful to me and played a very important part in my career by getting me a copy of Gray's *Anatomy*. Also my mother was your best friend, Sheshu said. (By the way, Mrs. Neilson, Sheshu lost his mother, and his father has remarried, and poor Sheshu and his sister are having some stepmother problems. But that is a big story in itself, and I will not trouble you with those details.) Anyway, Vimalamma, I must tell you something very important, Sheshu continued. I was recently in Tirupathi and I saw your husband there. He was with a very big tall American. The American gentleman had a forest of red hair on his head and was carrying a tape recorder and a big long camera. Your husband has grown a thick beard and is wearing dark sunglasses all the time. I was in Tirupathi for five days and I saw your husband talking to different sadhus. I could not control my curiosity, so I approached your husband, asked him what he was doing, when he returned from America, how you were, and other assorted questions. He told me that he was helping the American gentleman in his research about Indian sadhus and asked me not to tell you or anyone that he had been seen in Tirupathi, and then requested me to take some sacred *prassadam* to be given to his mother in Yalakki. I told him that I was not returning to Yalakki but proceeding directly to Vellore. Your husband again asked me not to tell anyone that I had seen him, particularly not you.

Then he said that if I followed his instructions, he would help me get a scholarship to go to America for higher studies in the field of medicine, maybe even in heart surgery. I thanked him and left.

Thus Sheshu reported to me about his meeting with my husband. Listening to Sheshu's story, I wept both out of joy and sadness. Joy because Kittu's father was still alive, and sad that our lives should be like a game of hide-and-seek.

After Sheshu left, I stayed at the temple for some time. Something told me that night that my husband would ultimately return to Yalakki.

I decided to wait with my usual patience. I had, for ten to twelve months, a period of terrible times for me and for my son Kittu. But we survived. I made pickles, *papadams*, *chatnipudi*, and other varieties of such food and sold them to various homes, a sort of one-woman business corporation. So you see, Mrs. Neilson, your group sponsoring me was not a total failure. I rented out my husband's room to a student. The proceeds from all this, however, kept our body and soul alive.

Then about seven or eight months ago a friend of my first brother, who was a former policeman, was returning on the Bangalore to Yalakki bus. This friend of my first brother saw my husband on the same bus. Even though it was after midnight, he immediately came and told my brother that he had watched my husband get off at the three-rock stop. Usually no one stops at three-rock stop, particularly at nighttime. Three-rock stop is close to cremation grounds. Not far from this is the deserted Cobra Temple, the same temple we took you to see the sadhu that Wednesday evening while you were here.

I was very surprised that my husband would go there, because there are all kinds of supernatural stories associated with that temple and people are afraid to go there at night. Do you remember that lifelike image of the black marble cobra in the center of the courtyard of the temple? I hope that the photo you took of it has come out nicely. One of the beliefs is that the cobra comes to life at night and moves around the temple courtyard, even moving down the stone steps to the river itself. Usually some milk mixed with honey is left in small bowls by various people during daytime for the cobra. In the morning not a drop is left. If by any chance a bowl is left with milk and honey, untouched, the belief is something bad will happen to the person to whom that bowl belongs because that person had not left the milk and honey with a pure heart. Of course my husband does not believe in all this. Blind, idiotic superstition is the way he has dismissed all these stories. I believe in all this. God works in mysterious ways unknown to man or woman. Being a deeply religious person, you will I am sure agree with me. Am I not right, Mrs. Neilson?

My brother came and woke me and decided first to go and inform the astrologer about the arrival of my husband. Then we thought to go very early in the morning and find out if the so-called person seen by the ex-policeman was really my husband. We will catch him while he is asleep and surprise him, my first brother said. The astrologer disagreed. Even though the astrologer deals with stars, planets, sun, moon, and so on, he is a very practical person. Before he became an astrologer, he was a lawyer, so he has a good mixture of both earthly and heavenly matters. It is my luck to have his advice and help.

The astrologer said, if your husband is posing as a sadhu, then he will have made a lot of money. Religion is big business. Like in all big business, in religion too there are crooks. They are the ones who give the noble profession of religion a very bad smell. Your husband is one such example. He has exploited the simple faith of our poor people, the majority of whom cannot tell the difference between what is genuine and what is artificial. Even if they are able to tell the difference, they are afraid to speak out.

The astrologer continued and said, Vimalamma, you and your son have suffered. The money that your husband has grabbed from innocent people under bogus appearance will not stay with him. Easy come, easy go. It goes to you. That is how your husband will meet divine justice. But you must be patient. I have a plan which you must follow.

I completely agreed with him and promised him that I would give him some contribution when everything turned out successful.

You do not have to give me too much, just enough to keep body and soul together so that I can serve mankind as long as possible, the astrologer said with his usual humility.

Around four A.M. all three of us went to the deserted Cobra Temple. A man was sleeping. He had covered himself in a sheet, so we were unable to verify whether the sheet-covered man was my husband or not.

We came away. The astrologer outlined his plan, which was that he and I would return to the deserted Cobra Temple about an hour or so later and sit close to where the sheet-covered man was sleeping. We would carry on a conversation in whispers, but loud enough for the sheet-covered man to hear.

Accordingly, we returned to the temple and enacted our drama. Because I do not want to bore you with too many details, I will give you the main points of our conversation. The astrologer said, Your husband is in America. He has a lot of money. By performing special ceremonies, I can influence several planets to have that money released to you. I replied by saying that I agreed with him, but I had no money to give him for the various ceremonies. Sell your jewelry, your husband's foreign-made typewriter, and even your house. I can get a good price for the house from Shetty, said the astrologer.

For your information, Mrs. Neilson, Shetty is the second richest man in Yalakki. On the outside he is a very charitable person who has donated to schools and temples. But on the backside he carries a very profitable moneylending business with high interest rates. Sometimes bad must support good, I think.

After this conversation between the astrologer and me which lasted for nearly an hour, we left the deserted Cobra Temple and walked down to the edge of the river. Soon we will know, said the astrologer, whether our drama will be successful or not in telling us what his plans are. After instructing me how to perform the second act of the drama and wishing me good luck, the astrologer left.

I sat on a stone step wondering how everything would turn out. I am not sure how long I sat there, but I woke up suddenly because I had fallen asleep and was about to fall off the step. I heard the splashing of water by a person in the river. There he was, my husband standing in front of me, not too far away, his back facing me! He was performing his ablutions.

No doubt!

He was my husband!

His hair reached to his shoulders.

He had become a bit fatter.

116

I became nervous all of a sudden and doubtful if I could keep calm and carry out the instructions given by the astrologer. I got up and walked away to control myself.

Walk in front of your husband, slowly, with your head bowed, as though you are in deep thought. Let him notice you. If he asks, Do you know who I am? you must answer, You are Swamiji. You are one who knows everything, past, present and future. These are the instructions that the astrologer had given me.

I was not certain if I could say all those words without laughing. But I decided to try. So I slowly walked toward my husband. He was now sitting by the edge of the river, submerged in water up to his waist. After I had passed him, he said, You are in great worry.

I stopped. The way he said those words, like he was a real sadhu who had powers to look into the past and the future, made me laugh. I muffled my laughter by covering my mouth with the flap of my sari.

My husband thought I had started to sob.

God sends troubles only to man. It is his way of testing our faith, my husband philosophised.

If he keeps up like this, it will be very difficult for me to control my anger and my laughter, I thought. I stood still and started to cough in order to conceal my laughter.

You have traveled across oceans. Your troubles began there. Now you want to get back your husband, my husband continued.

I felt I had to say something, so I took a deep breath and turned to face him. He was wearing dark glasses, and just as Sheshu said, there was a big scar on his forehead.

What do you know of my troubles? I asked as innocently and as reverently as I could.

He turned his face away from me, and looking across the river asked, Is it not true what I am saying?

It is, it is. That is why I am asking, I said, taking a step toward my husband.

He stood up from the water and turned his back to me. Then he said, Do not listen to pretenders. Your husband will send for you. He is very much interested in your welfare. He is a very good man. He is very intelligent. But like all great men, sometimes he is not recognised for his true intelligence.

I listened to this self-certificate he was giving himself. I hope he is safe, I said. You act all right, but I can act better than you, I said to myself.

What is safe? Is anything permanent? he asked.

He has really learned how to double-talk, how to answer a question with another question, I thought. Continue, continue. I will give you a very long rope. You pretend, all right. I can pretend better than you, I said to myself.

But I want to caution you. Do not act hastily. Good times will come. Have faith, trust, he said.

I have faith. I have trust. But how long can I continue like this, I asked.

He did not reply immediately but looked up at the sky, then lowered his head as though he were seriously thinking. Then he said, Two days from now, just before sunrise, go to the well in your neighbour's house. Around the well wall there is a missing brick. In that place there will be a sign which will give you assurance that your husband is thinking of you and your son.

Ah, Swamiji, you know everything. You know about my son too, I said. By now my acting had really improved!

My husband looked at the sky as though telling me that God reveals all this knowledge to him.

What is this sign in the missing brick hole in the well wall? I asked.

He shook his head and ended the conversation. I bowed to him.

He raised his right hand over my head and blessed me and then came out of the river and walked up the steps to the temple courtyard. He was certainly much fatter now. Almost roly-poly, like you Americans describe a plump person.

Why is he doing all this? How long will he continue? What is his ultimate purpose? I wondered. I have never been able to understand my husband from the day I married him. He has said that he has never understood me. So why should we understand each other now?

But I am still his wife, the mother of his son. Besides, Mrs. Neilson, I become very sad if I see anyone without food. So I decided that I should go to my house and prepare some food. Also, my cooking he has always praised. After some time I returned with food, fruits, and some milk. My first brother came with me.

My husband was inside the temple sanctuary.

I stood outside the door and said, Swamiji, please take some food.

My brother joined in my request. I spread a green banana leaf, sprinkled some water on it, put all the food vessels near it and said, Swamiji, everything is ready.

I am meditating. Do not disturb me, please go, my husband said.

We left, but took position outside the temple courtyard by crouching on the ground and watched.

My husband came out of the temple sanctuary and looked around. He first picked up the brass jar with the lid, thinking it was coffee. After he opened and found out that it was milk, his face contorted in disgust. Then he sat down to feast on my food.

My brother and I tiptoed away and returned home. The astrologer joined us a bit later and heard our report. Let us be patient, he suggested.

Late in the evening I returned to the deserted Cobra Temple with some fruits. My husband was sitting and praying, wearing his dark glasses. Whether he was doing this because he saw me coming or whether he was really praying I am not certain.

I sat quietly near one of the stone pillars, watching him.

About twenty or twenty-five minutes later he slowly turned his face in my direction.

I bowed and said, I have some fresh fruits, and offered them.

He nodded and reached out and took a banana.

Tell me about your son, he asked as he peeled the banana.

I answered. Then he went on asking many questions about my mother-in-law and his sisters and so on, all in a very indirect way. I must say he was very clever in asking these questions and getting all the answers. I told him the truth, that my mother-in-law was now in Kolar with her daughter Shuba, and so on and so forth, giving him a full report.

After he had satisfied his hunger for information about his mother and kith and kin, he once again told me, Do not listen to bogus astrologers. They will take everything you own.

I thanked him, bowed, touched his feet, gathered up all the vessels, and returned home.

Thursday morning before sunrise I went to my neighbour's well. On the brick wall, there was a loose brick. I removed it. There were one hundred rupees!

We—that is my brother, astrologer, and myself—knew right away that my husband had come there sometime in the dark and left that money to prove to me his supernatural powers.

Actually, Mrs. Neilson, I shed tears. I wanted to go to my husband and tell him, Please listen to me. I know who you are. Why all this pretension?

But my brother and the astrologer persuaded me not to do so. They were convinced that my husband had a secret plan for being in Yalakki. Let him confess if he wants to. You play the game. Act out the drama. Do not be foolish because of your basic sympathetic nature. Did he not pretend to be in import-export business? Then did he not pretend to be mad? Now he is pretending to be a saint, sadhu, holy man, guruji, swamiji, etc., etc. What next? So be cautious. Collect as much money as you can. You have a son to consider. Further, for society's sake he must be exposed for who he is, they advised me.

In the meanwhile word spread in our town that a swamiji had appeared, that he had magical powers to tell people where they can find money. So people began to visit him. A few at first, then lots and lots of them. You yourself saw what a lot of people there were. Long lines all the time.

My swamiji husband was upset by all this publicity and asked me why I had spread word about his existence.

I did not, I told him.

Then who? he asked.

I told him I did not know who it was.

But I knew that it was the astrologer who had spread the word. Because my husband had tried to expose the astrologer by telling me not to listen to pretenders, the astrologer wanted to expose my husband in a very public, very humiliating manner. A simple case of tit for tat.

To get himself some privacy, my husband recruited a young beggar boy by the name of Subbu to guard the door and control the crowd.

He had, however, instructed Subbu that whenever I arrived, I must be given immediate entry. This he did, not because of any love for me, but because I brought him my home-cooked food. The crowds of people always brought my husband, the holy man, bananas, coconuts, milk, rock candy, sugarcane, flowers, etc., etc. Sometimes my husband gave me some of these items to take home. I know that he sent coconuts with Subbu to be sold to one of the restaurants in town, when no one was looking. Of course, some of this money from the sale of coconuts came to me indirectly, because my husband left it in hidden places like the loose brick opening in the well wall. Only once there was no money left in the place where he had said it would be. I realised why, because my husband had been unable to sneak out and hide the money because of the large crowds in front of the temple.

I have not told Kittu that the swamiji in the temple is his father. I took Kittu with me twice and he bowed and touched his father's feet and was blessed and given five rupees each time.

How strange. Why all this? Is my husband really mad and thinks he is a genuine sadhu? I kept asking myself over and over.

Although I could see the reasoning behind the arguments of my brother and the astrologer to continue my acting, I felt sympathy for my husband. After all he is my husband, the father of my son. So I decided that the next time I had some privacy with him I would tell him that I knew who he was, that he should give up all this pretension and return to his house and we could begin afresh.

Frankly, all this taking food back and forth, this continuous acting, all the crowds of people had begun to upset me very much. I began to have bad dreams.

One dream in particular was very bad. In this dream the crowd exposed my husband to be a bogus sadhu and I was accused as his copartner in this scheme to exploit poor innocent people. Both my husband and I were put in prison. Outside the prison poor Kittu sobbed uncontrollably. I woke up screaming and decided that I would see my husband the following day and tell him to put an end to this stupid drama.

It was Friday morning. I went early. As I approached the deserted Cobra Temple, as usual crowds were beginning to gather. I saw a car in front of the temple and a khaki-uniformed driver standing by it. I immediately recognised the car as belonging to Keshava Moorthy, the richest man in Yalakki. So, I thought, my husband's fame has spread and he is getting deeper and deeper into a mess. Then I saw a lady walk down the temple steps and stop to put on her slippers, which she had left at the entrance. The driver opened the car door, she got in the car. He closed the door, got in the front seat. The car left.

I recognised the lady. She was Saroja, my husband's secret sweetheart. I entered the temple, determined more than ever to tell the truth. As usual, Subbu made a way for me and opened the door of my husband's sanctuary. I bowed and placed the food in front of him.

My fame has spread, he said, and asked, Do you know who was here just before you arrived?

No, I said.

The daughter of Yalakki's richest man, he announced proudly with great happiness.

Saroja? I asked.

Yes, Saroja, he said as though he was making love to the name itself. She has beauty, wealth, everything, he continued.

But she is barren as the desert. She has no child, I said.

That is why she was here! he said, his mouth breaking into a big smile. Doctors, astrologers, sadhus she has consulted, gone on pilgrimages, but no avail. Now she has come to me.

Control yourself! Do not do something that will land you in more trouble, I wanted to say. But he was like a drunken man, in seventh heaven, because she had come to see him.

Do you know that one time she was in love with me? he asked.

Who? Saroja? I asked innocently.

He nodded very confidently.

So you have been in Yalakki before? I asked.

A long time ago, very long time ago, not here actually, only passing through, he corrected himself and started to cough, realising he had made a mistake.

Can you give her a child? I asked.

If I make up my mind, I can, he said.

Will you make up your mind? I asked.

I am thinking, he said, then added, I can do it.

I realised then that he had actually begun to believe he really had supernatural powers.

How will you give her a baby? I wanted to ask. Sprinkle some water on her stomach? Ask her to close her eyes and say that some spirit is going to make her pregnant, do some hanky-panky, like some bogus sadhus? Now I wholeheartedly agreed with my brother and astrologer that my husband had to be exposed in the grand manner to make him humble! I decided to let him perspire.

Then he said, From tonight you don't have to bring me any food because Saroja has made arrangements to have food sent to me through her driver. As you know, they have excellent cooks in their house.

I got up, forced myself to touch his feet and, controlling my anger and tears, came out.

So the days continued. I became very restless and anxious, not knowing what exactly to do next.

In the meanwhile when I went to visit him again and told him about my financial difficulties and how I thought of selling my house, he was not interested at all. He had come under the magic spell of his secret sweetheart, Saroja. I even thought of approaching Saroja and telling her who the swamiji was. It was then that your letter arrived announcing your intended arrival. I was so happy that you were coming. I decided to tell my husband about your arrival and test his reaction.

I went to see him with your letter and told him that my husband had received a letter from America, and I wanted his advice.

Who has written the letter? What does it say? he asked.

I told him.

This American woman, she must not come, he said, becoming very agitated. Time not auspicious. Planetary conjunctions not proper. It will upset all calculations I am doing to have your husband send for you and your son to join him in America, he added very sternly.

So you want me to write and ask her not to come? I asked.

Yes, yes, definitely, he said. Even send cable, he urged, and asked me to leave the letter with him.

I did and returned home, keeping only the envelope with your address on it, saying Kittu wants American stamps.

My brother, astrologer, and myself decided that we would not write you, and of course definitely not send you a cable. We wanted you to come. We decided to take you to the deserted Cobra Temple where you could recognise my husband and expose him in front of all the people.

But man proposes, God disposes.

When we took you to see him, he had already found out that you had arrived and he knew you were waiting to see him, probably even going to take a picture of him with your camera. Subbu was the one who told him that a white American woman was outside with me. So my husband instructed Subbu to announce no darshan today—Swamiji in samadhi. Swamiji in fear, trembling, and perspiring would have been closer to the truth!

Naturally, we were very disappointed. Several times on the way back to the hotel, I thought of telling you the whole story. When we met you at the Yalakki railway station, the first question you asked was, Where is Raj? I replied, Oh, he had to go on some urgent college business. He is very sorry to have missed you. Diplomatically, you did not press the question. Maybe you understood that something was wrong. Returning to the hotel, I was tempted to say, Mrs. Neilson, I am sorry I told you a lie when you arrived. The true answer to your question is, my husband is ... , and then tell you the entire story which I have now written you. But how would I have convinced you? We would have had to go back to the deserted Cobra Temple and try to expose him. All that would have been a mess in the presence of a guest like yourself. So again, out of politeness and good manners, I kept silent.

Then my husband attempted to enter your hotel room. The rest you know.

Anyway, I went to the post office, as I was telling you at the start, to post that short letter, and the postal clerk looked at the address. He said, Oh, another letter to the same person and same address?

Another letter? Same person? Same address? Mrs. Nielson? America? Who wrote her? I asked, already knowing who it might be.

Cannot answer because there was no from address, only to, the postal clerk replied.

Are you certain? I asked.

Absolutely certain. Cent percent certain. Same person, same address, same U.S.A. I have a good memory. Good memory is a required qualification for postal clerks, he said.

Can you tell me who brought that other letter? I asked.

A beggar boy, he said.

With that information it did not need double 07 James Bond to detect it was Subbu who brought the letter. To guarantee that it was Subbu, my first brother approached him. Gave him two rupees. Subbu told everything: that Swamiji tried to see American woman in hotel room, that Swamiji sat up all night writing long long letter to American woman, that he, Subbu, took the letter to be posted. Please do not tell Swamiji that I told you all this, Subbu begged my brother.

By now, Mrs. Neilson, you have received the long letter from my husband. Contents of that I do not know. What I have written is the truth. My husband has probably written you asking you to help him return to America. My humble request is, please, Mrs. Neilson, do not help him. Do not again put yourself to all that trouble of raising all the money, all that planning, etc., etc., to get him to America.

My husband says he is swamiji with supernatural powers. He says he can do anything if he makes up his mind. He has miraculous powers, he says. If he has all this, then let him use his mental powers to loom a magic carpet, simply, simply, just like that, and fly to America!

One thing I will tell you, Mrs. Neilson. This time my husband will not vanish in the middle of the night or in the early morning, or anytime. I will surround him with the entire population of Yalakki. I will spread the word about his supernatural powers. I will tell everyone that I have found money because of his powers.

Crowds, enormous crowds, not only of Yalakki, but from other towns, will come and surround him, to get his darshan. Day and night, he will be surrounded by people.

His protector of privacy, Subbu, is already in the pay of my first brother and is keeping us informed of every move my husband makes. My brother is thinking of going to Bangalore and getting a newspaper reporter to visit Yalakki.

This time my husband, His Holiness Swamiji of Yalakki, cannot escape.

I am sorry to pour out all my troubles to you, but I do not want to be tricked again.

Please write and tell me that you have received my letter. Please tell me that you will not come to the aid of my husband.

If you are interested, I will keep you informed of what happens to my husband as the crowds congregate in Yalakki and move closer and closer to the deserted Cobra Temple.

My son Kittu sends you his love and greetings.

Mrs. Neilson, you must come again to Yalakki after this is over. I must give you proper hospitality next time.

Your sincere and beloved friend,
Vimala

I put down the letter, exhausted from all the maneuvers, moves, and countermoves these two antagonists were directing at each other. Then I started giggling. Theater of the absurd, Indian-style, was all I could think of.

When I finally called Thelma to talk to her about the two letters, she said, "Wait, there are two more!"

"What?"

"Yes, I received them yesterday. One from each. They're quite short. Want me to read them to you?"

"Do I!"

"OK. Raj's first."

"Dear Mrs. Neilson, I am eagerly waiting for your letter concerning sponsorship by The One and Only. Also your thank-you-for-your-hospitality letter to my wife is eagerly expected. I hope it will contain the code word I mentioned so that I can get some peace of mind. As Hamlet says, 'I will by indirections find directions out' when your letter reaches my wife. The situation here is getting heated up. Your help desperately needed. Your son in deep trouble, Raj."

"In deep what?" I said and started giggling again. "Thelma, these two people are totally out to lunch."

"Oh, but now listen to Vimala's. She's a vixen."

"Dear Mrs. Neilson, I hope you have received my letter. Sorry to have made you take so much of your valuable time in reading it. My husband is telling me that I am responsible for imprisoning him in this crowd of people. I must get rid of them. He needs peace and privacy. A sadhu must have time to meditate and concentrate, he says, so that he can help me in achieving my desires. If I want my husband to send for me and my son to America, then get rid of these crowds, he says. Tell your brother, he says, not to bring any newspaper reporter to get me publicity; I do not want it.

"I know why he wants the crowds to dissolve. He wants to escape. Mrs. Neilson, I am not interested in coming to America. It is nothing personal against you. If my husband wants to flee to America, let him grow wings and fly. I hope I am clear. With my best wishes and the best wishes of my son Kittu and my first brother, your sincere and beloved friend, Vimala."

"Well, she's certainly got him by the. . . ." Whoops, I thought, Thelma's pretty straitlaced, better watch it.

"Poor Raj," Thelma said.

"You know what, Thelma?"

"What?"

"I think I agree more with Vimala than with Raj."

"Well . . . but I do feel sorry for him. I've got a plan that I think will enable him to come to America, if he can only get out of Vimala's clutches."

When I finally put down the phone, I sat for some time looking out the window. I was beginning to wonder if Thelma's head was screwed on any tighter than those of Raj and his wife. But she *did* have a plan, and what's more, it would probably work if Raj could, as she put it, get out of Vimala's clutches.

PART FOUR

○ ○ ○

THE HOLY
HEIST

1

My dear Mrs. Neilson:

I am just like a yo-yo. That is my honest answer to your simple question: "Raj, how are you?"

So much has happened during the course of these past four to five hours that I am dizzy with delight and despair. My head is literally swimming. I've been bounced up and down, high and low, emotionally that is, so that I'm not sure where or how to begin this letter to you.

Quite some time ago I wrote you a rather lengthy letter. It was more than a letter. It was a naked, uninhibited, desperate cry of a son in trouble, seeking help from his mother. In more ways than one, you are my mother.

"Raj, I am your American mother. And I mean that!" How many times did you not say that to me while I was in Avalon? Answer:

countless times. I accepted it then. I accept it now. I do believe, since I am a firm believer in the theory of reincarnation, that we were, you and I, mother and son in a previous life. Incidentally, my mother, the one who facilitated my entry into this life, quietly drifted off in her sleep into that land from where no traveler has as yet returned. One good thing being that when my mother commenced that nonreturnable journey, she was in my sister's house who also happened to be her favorite daughter. Incidentally as a footnote, let me say that my sister is expecting and, therefore, it is possible, rather I should say probable, that my dear departed mother's soul might return as my sister's daughter.

Death comes to all and life is but an illusion, fundamental facts of existence we must all accept.

I have shed my tears, so let me proceed. Much has happened since I last wrote you. Much awaits to happen. In that letter I shared with you how I had been inadvertently trapped into the somewhat embarrassing predicament of playing the holy man, reluctantly, and how I had expected my performance in this role to be temporary. However, much to my disappointment it has turned out to be a long run. There's the rub!

In my letter of ancient vintage, I pleaded for a speedy response from you. I begged you to get in touch with The One and Only group in Los Angeles to help me extricate myself from this awkward situation. Since you are, according to your own self-description, a packet rat who does not throw away anything, you might still have that letter. If you do, I think you do, I respectfully urge you to read it once more. You will then see how I prostrated myself, metaphorically that is, and asked you to communicate through a code, in a letter to my wife, so as to restore a semblance of tranquility to my troubled heart.

Dead silence on your part.

Believe me, this is no accusation, Mrs. Neilson. You too are a part of the human condition and, I realise, have your ups and downs. I merely state a fact.

Day in and day out, I waited anxiously for your response. But I was doomed to disappointment. If only you knew the hundreds of letters I mentally composed to you, each and every night, you'd be astonished. But I have no regrets in composing those unwritten and therefore naturally unposted letters.

Even though these unwritten letters never reached you, they constituted my hope for living. My lifeline, so to speak. They provided the needed strength to survive each day. Without such mental composing, that imaginary conversation with you, during my periods of so-called serene, rapturous meditation—eyes closed and mind presumably empty of all the clutter of daily living—I would have simply died. Simply, simply expired, Mrs. Neilson. That is no exaggeration.

I am still lodged in the temple premises—under house arrest more appropriately describes my present status.

You, of course, visited the temple in the company of my wife when you were here. You came to the temple vicinity in the cool of the evening. When I heard that you were out there among the congregation, I canceled my regular *darshana* to my devotees. I could not bear to see you and not welcome you to my hometown about which I had waxed so eloquently and poetically to you in Avalon. Tranquil, pastoral Yalakki by the banks of the babbling brook, so cool, so idyllic, the image I had conjured up. Nostalgia, fantasy, and a touch of romanticism all blended to create that image.

There is no such thing as "cool" anymore in Yalakki. It is hot, very hot. Sizzling, simmering heat, day and night. It is one of those "break an egg and you have a cooked omelette in your palms" kinds of heat; or "hold a cup of water and it will boil and bubble for a cup of tea" kinds of heat. Heatwise, we are in the suffocating grip of a prolonged drought. Today is the forty-first day of this horrendous H_2O famine.

The babbling brook no longer babbles. It is dry and cracked. The babbling is only from the crowds of people who have gathered here. They have come from everywhere. Far and near, young and old, men and women, children and pregnant girls, rich and poor, strong and weak, the devout and the merely curious. In a nutshell, the entire spectrum of humanity representing every aspect of the human condition has gathered and continues to gather in front of the Cobra Temple.

I have become the object of their adoration and hope. The cynosure of their eyes! It frightens me. The sense of fear increases when I realize the awesome responsibility I have shouldered, the faith and belief of all these people. I realise that the moment of truth is fast approaching. My predicament has become even more precarious. The noose around my neck is getting tighter. The high noon of my show-down is fast approaching. The showdown between me and—you guessed it right—my wife.

This showdown which I dread is scheduled for Sunday, two days from today. It is expected to take place in front of thousands of people.

Let me explain how I was unwittingly lured to put my head in this tightening noose.

My wife knows who I am. She wants to expose me. I want to escape from her. These are the bare essentials of the plot of the drama now taking place. These are blunt truths. She is aided by her deceitful brother. That is her advantage over me. I am straightforward and simple and all alone. I am therefore at a serious disadvantage.

Anyway, let me get to the point. My wife has gradually and somewhat surreptitiously worked herself into the position of what you might call the keeper of the gates to the temple sanctuary behind which I am lodged. She has become a sort of unofficial hostess. She has projected herself as a woman who has access to my ears—my confidante, my alter ego, my protector. Of course, the gullible public just eats it up, hook, line, and sinker.

My wife not only controls the vast crowds gathered in front of the Cobra Temple, but also shrewdly and diabolically controls even my exits and entrances to and from the sanctuary. She tells Subbu, my gofer, when to tell me to come out of my sanctuary to appear before the public and when to return to the womb of the sanctuary.

Amazing, Mrs. Neilson, just amazing what this wife of mine has achieved. She could easily write a book on mind control and body movement. When I realised how I had been turned into a puppet in her hands, and by implication in the hands of her brother who con-trols her, I became angry, disgusted and, far worse, depressed.

So, one evening approximately two weeks ago, I decided to take a stand. The crowds had gathered, and I could hear the frenzied chanting by the crowds, "Govinda, Govinda," the name of the Lord, led, of course, by none other than my wife. Subbu came and announced that it was time for me to make my appearance.

"No!" I said.

"No? But Guruji . . ." he started.

"No!" I replied forcefully. "Go. Depart," I ordered him. "I'm in samadhi." Mrs. Neilson, *samadhi* means serious meditation, a state of being where body, mind, and soul are all perfectly united to create maximum concentration, a sort of suspended animation.

Subbu hesitated but left.

Then after half an hour or so, I heard a loud announcement through the megaphone, which is like your public address system. It was, of course, the voice of my wife. "I have to announce to all of you both good news and bad news," she was saying. "We will not be able to have Guruji's darshana for seven days. We cannot see him face-to-face as we have been doing all these days. Why can we not see him? The answer is as follows: for our welfare, for the welfare of our whole country Guruji is undertaking a seven-day fast. He will pray and perform *tapas*, enter samadhi, carry on *dhyana*. All this in order to bring forth the much needed rain. He wants to chase this famine from our land. Banish it forever.

"After seven days Guruji will appear and announce to all of us when the rains will arrive and thereby end this famine."

What is she up to? I wondered. Who authorised her to make this announcement? I wanted to rush out and literally strangle her. Oh, Mrs. Neilson, I became indescribably angry.

By now the entire crowd, there must have been thousands, had broken into vociferous chanting. The very air was rent with the frenzied chanting of God's name, "Govinda, Govinda," interspersed with devotion for me, "Guruji, Guruji."

Announcement on the eighth day of the time and day of the coming of rains?

My wife had gone crazy. Gone nuts. Bananas.

By speaking for me, without my permission, which, of course, the crowds did not know, she had trapped me. I was imprisoned. Once again she had tightened her control over me.

I waited to pounce on Subbu and rid my anger on him. However, he never showed up until the next morning. He had no doubt joined my wife and feasted with her while I was left to starve.

But I did not starve. I innovated. I improvised. There were a few devotees among the hundreds who came to visit the temple, who continued to leave food, fruits, and a tumbler of milk on a stone slab that jutted out from the right side of the temple wall. These offerings were ostensibly for Nagappa, King Cobra, who, as I told you before, according to legend and belief lay within the temple precincts. I had done nothing to destroy that belief. In the dark of the night I became Nagappa, the King Cobra, and consumed the food. I would not give my wife the satisfaction of my silent starvation. I decided that I would emerge on the eighth day and publicly denounce my wife for her announcement made without my knowledge or permission. My defiance made me feel much better.

For want of time let me skip the seven days.

I emerged on the eighth day and gazed upon the sea of faces. My wife bowed and touched my feet and smiled, reminding me of Shakespeare's immortal words: "Smile and smile and yet be a villain." Even her satanic brother bowed to me, which reminded me of Shakespeare's "et tu, Brute?" It may not be the most appropriate quote but I think you get the drift of what I'm trying to say. He then handed to my wife the megaphone.

She addressed the crowd and flattered me. Gross, unadulterated, downright deceitful flattery. It made me sick.

I could no longer tolerate her hypocrisy. I raised my hands to stop her. When she ignored me, I simply raised my voice and spoke, amazed at the strength and sound of my own voice.

"Devotees of Yalakki, listen," I began. "You have been deceived. Yes, grossly and unjustly deceived."

There was pindrop silence in that vast sea of simple but innocent humanity. Each and every one literally hung upon each and every word I spoke. I was both impressed and deeply touched by the respect and attention I received from thousands of people while my own wife and son ignored me.

"I did not say that I would announce today when the rains would come. Only God has that knowledge. . . ."

136

"But Guruji," my wife interrupted, "You have prayed to God. God has talked to you."

The crowd roared their approval by chanting:

"Govinda, Govinda . . . Guruji, Guruji."

My wife whipped them into even more frenzied chanting.

"Guruji, you have the power to end this drought. You have the power. You have demonstrated to me many times your power by telling me where to look for money. I followed your advice and found money. So Guruji, please help us. Please," she begged as crocodile tears flowed from her eyes. Then she urged the vast crowd to do likewise.

The entire crowd went down on their knees with folded hands. The chanting again started: "Guruji, Guruji, Guruji, Guruji."

She asked the crowd to stop and she spoke. "Guruji, we will follow your path of purity and honesty. It will be difficult for us. But you have set a shining example. If our hearts and minds are cleansed, under your guidance, your direction, your shining everlasting leadership, then rain will pour upon our dry and parched, starved and thirsty earth. So please, Guruji, help us. Nothing is impossible to you," she begged.

Then she again started a frenzied chanting, as she swayed back and forth, urging the crowd to do likewise.

Oh, Mrs. Neilson, what a show she put on!

How, tell me how, Mrs. Neilson, could I say no to these thousands of people?

If I exposed myself as a fake holy man to these thousands of believers, would I not jeopardise the reputation of men who are truly holy? I hope you understand my reasoning, Mrs. Neilson.

The sound of their chanting and the excruciating heat of the afternoon both combined to give me a splitting headache. I ached all over just to be left alone. I wanted to scream: "Go on. Disperse, get lost. Leave me alone."

Instead of saying those words and as though propelled by forces stronger than me, I found myself raising my hands to silence the crowd. Gradually the chanting subsided. The intensity of my headache increased. Without any preamble, I simply announced: "Next

Sunday, the rains will come." I bowed to the crowds and returned to my sanctuary.

Even as I walked the few steps to my refuge within the Cobra Temple, I realised that I had entered a tight cage. My wife had done it openly, publicly. She had done it with respect, devotion, and the applause of my devotees. She lifted the door of one trap and made me walk into a tighter trap.

The crowds continued their chanting for several hours. My impulsive prediction of rainfall had intensified my predicament. I cancelled my darshanas for the following days and announced through Subbu that my next appearance would be on Sunday, the forty-third day of the drought, the day it would end.

Sunday is only two days away.

Aided, abetted, and assisted by her eldest brother, my wife has spread the news of the promised rain. To watch the performance of the miracle, to experience it as *tamasha*, which really means a fun sort of thing, my wife has launched a massive campaign to gather as many people as possible. She wants to get newspaper reporters from Bangalore. She is determined to pull the noose tight around my neck in public. To be quite frank, Mrs. Neilson, the very thought of the fast approaching Sunday makes me break into a cold sweat.

I have to get out of Yalakki before it comes.

My wife has everyone watching me. The old man with the wrinkled skin who sells coconuts at the entrance to the temple; the dark-eyed young girl who sells flowers that have wilted in this heat; the devotees who bring me their respects, are all unwittingly or wittingly my wife's informants. Under the guise of concern and compassion for my safety she has told all these people: "We must watch and protect Guruji every day, night and day. He is our treasure. Our brightest jewel. There are terrorists everywhere. No one must lure him out or kidnap him. So watch his every move and report to me. Follow him like a shadow."

She could easily teach the CIA, KGB, and MI-5 or is it MI-4, that British spy agency, and any other secret agencies, including the top-notch Israeli agency, a few new tricks.

Confidentially speaking, I cannot even trust Subbu. I think you might remember Subbu from your previous visit. He has become globular, a veritable butterball, round and plump. He continues, as I told you earlier, to be my gofer. I wish I could dump him and take someone else. But Subbu knows too much and is very familiar with what you might call skeletons in the closet. Who does not have a bone or two buried? That is why there is a saying in India: "Never trace the origins of a mighty river or the roots of a holy man." I think I might have mentioned to you this folk wisdom one time. If Subbu were in America, he would be the type who would ghostwrite one of those kiss-and-tell books. In his case it would be a never-kissed, yet-told type of a book, and make a million or more.

In the interests of pure self-survival, I have to be extremely diplomatic with him. I must think twice before I say anything. He believes that I will take him with me to America to continue to serve as my gofer. Frankly, I have neither said yes nor no. Why should I go out of my way to destroy his illusions? Illusions are necessary to face life's harsh realities.

Mrs. Neilson, I know I am digressing. But I had to set the stage so that you can better understand and sympathise with my opening statement that I am like a yo-yo.

To put it in another way, I am left swinging in the wind, slowly, very slowly.

Let me return to the events of this morning so as to establish some sort of chronological coherence.

Thinking of the approaching Sunday showdown, I was unable to sleep last night. The heat was indescribably unbearable. The Cobra Temple is not far from Yalakki's cremation grounds. Last night there were four or five cremations. The heat and smoke from the funeral pyres only added to the unsatisfactory physical and psychological environment.

Unable to sleep, I paced up and down. I composed one of my imaginary letters to you. It was more a conversation than a letter. Actually, it was a monologue.

About three or three-thirty in the morning I became extremely restless, so restless that I decided to escape from my prison without bars, at least to make an attempt. Nothing ventured, nothing gained,

I said to myself. If only I could somehow make my way to the cremation grounds, I reflected, I could then surreptitiously snake my way to the dry, bushes-covered backyard of Moorthy's mansion.

Moorthy, Mrs. Neilson, is Yalakki's wealthiest man. His mansion of many marvellous rooms, most of them mirrored, is one of the so-called "must see" items in Yalakki. Moorthy is currently out of Yalakki, on an all-India-Holy-Places pilgrimage and is not expected to return for another year or more. The mansion is occupied by his daughter Saroja and her husband, Subramanya Swami, nicknamed Mani for short. Mani also happens to be the only son of another wealthy man and has two automobiles, though one of them is old and often won't start, and like the vehicle of my wife's brother, the door on the passenger side is broken and won't open from the inside.

Both Mani and Saroja are beholden to me for some small favor I have done them. It is nothing to boast about, just humanity helping humanity. So let me not waste too much time on my minuscule favor. I believe in what you used to say so often from the Bible: "Let not your right hand know what your left hand has done." While I am quoting the Bible, let me go a step further and remember that other quote: "The truth shall make you free." Another favorite of yours. What I am trying to say to you, Mrs. Neilson, is that I once, indeed, had a crush on Saroja. I had been smitten by her fragile beauty, her grace. Since we are in the realm of truth, I was awed by her wealth also. So I admit my love for Sweet Saroja. And I suppose the embers of the fire from that past love still flicker, though they do not smoulder as they once did. There you have it, the truth, and the whole truth.

One more footnote, Mrs. Neilson, and I will move on to the more serious narration. That is, my wife will no doubt exaggerate my past love for Saroja. If she does, which she will, you will have already heard it from me, my conscience is clear. Now, back to my escape plan.

I knew that if I reached the back area of Moorthy's mansion, I could escape to Bangalore by hook or crook, and once in Bangalore I could easily get lost in the mass of unwashed millions.

Subbu was asleep. Snoring. Dead to the world.

I picked up my cloth bag containing my diaries, notes, reflections, and other assorted paraphernalia.

Hardly had I climbed down the last step of the temple to take my first step towards freedom, than I was approached by two young men, both brothers, named Shyamu and Ramu. Both of them belonging to the mother's-milk-scarce-yet-dry-upon-their-tender-lips type. Politely as they greeted me, words dripped with honey, full of eagerness to assist their beloved swamiji. I remembered Shakespeare again (see above): "Men can smile and smile and yet be villains." Shyamu and Ramu have traditionally led the chanting at the conclusion of my evening benediction.

But they did not fool me one minute. I saw right through them. They were as transparent as the diaphanous sari of a street prostitute! Sorry for being so blunt. My anger bubbles at this kind of hypocrisy. Forgive me.

There was no way I could get past them. They would stick to me like leeches. I mumbled something about excessive heat and the need for prayer and slowly climbed the steps back to my space in the temple.

I also knew that this feeble attempt at escape would be reported, probably magnified, to my wife and to her eldest brother. Security around me would be tightened.

I needed desperately to escape. There was no way I could do it by myself.

Three buckets of cold water, turned lukewarm by the time they reached me, had arrived by car from Moorthy's mansion. Since the drought Moorthy's mansion has supplied water for my morning ablutions. They have a special water pump which provides them with increased water.

I bathed. Subbu woke up and used part of the water for his ablutions. He prepared my morning coffee and then took off to Bhatta's Neo-Café to fetch me my breakfast.

Do you remember this café? It is practically next to the New Modern Hotel, where you stayed and unfortunately got frightened by me.

Bhatta's Neo-Café is an excellent eatery. Under normal circumstances I would have taken you out for an evening meal, a pure vegetarian delight served on a fresh green banana leaf, with all the fixings and the trimmings.

141

Neo-Café has been supplying me with breakfasts each morning. Their contribution to the good cause, so to speak.

But freedom was on my mind this morning, not breakfast.

I drank a second cup of coffee. I reflected intensely on how to extricate myself out of this pickle I'd gotten myself into, a pickling process assisted by my wife, of course—at which she is an expert in more ways than one. I even considered the drastic step of publicly confessing to the crowd on Sunday, asking their forgiveness.

But I quickly ruled that out. That would just put an end to my dreams of returning to America. It would also take away my chances of doing good to my people, making amends for my mistakes.

My proposed books on the life-styles of holy men, my TV appearances, my spiritual consultation services—all organized and developed in Avalon, America, under your guidance—could result in handsome financial returns. It's been proved over and over that religion is a surefire money-maker. I would, of course, channel part of these funds for development projects in Yalakki. Schools and maybe even a college could be established. Irrigation equipment, etc., etc. Human needs are simply endless.

I would also be providing an opportunity for those altruistic Americans to assist in the development of Third-World nations.

This would be my penance. My mea culpa.

My plan may seem rather rough. Believe me, I have it all worked out to the last detail in my mind. I am only summarising the bare essentials to save time. I hope you understand.

To accomplish these noble tasks I must return to Avalon. It is as simple, as direct, and, unfortunately, as complex as that.

Subbu returned from Neo-Café with the aluminum breakfast carrier. Actually, he sort of stumbled in. He was out of breath and profusely perspiring. He started to blabber. I thought that some indescribable calamity had fallen upon him. I tried to calm him down and after a few minutes he collected his thoughts and said that while he was at the Neo-Café, he had found out that Robbed American Woman had arrived and taken a room at the New Modern Hotel.

That bit of news startled, surprised, and delighted me.

Believe me, I too started to blabber. I literally wanted to scream for joy. I felt like jumping up and down. Subbu's face was a massive grin from ear to ear. Tears of joy poured from my eyes. After some moments of this unspeakable kind of elation, I asked Subbu to repeat what he had heard. "Say it slowly," I commanded him.

"Robbed American Woman has arrived in Yalakki and taken a room in the New Modern Hotel," he said.

I asked him to repeat it three times. He did.

By the way, Mother Neilson, you are Robbed American Woman. That is how you are referred to in Yalakki. It is not meant in any way to be insulting. It is their way of showing continued sympathy for the plight you fell into, caused inadvertently, as you know, by me. Once again my apologies.

Mrs. Neilson, I cannot adequately express my joy at this bit of stupendous news. A million questions crowded my mind. Escape, freedom was at hand, I believed.

My restlessness increased because I wanted to see you right away. I ignored my favorite breakfast of *masala dosai*. You might recall that I had once fixed that eatable for ten members of your church for a fund-raiser at your home for breakfast. You loved it. They loved it. You ate two of my pancakes stuffed with spicy vegetables.

I will be glad to repeat this or any other fund-raiser your heart desires for you and your friends. Bhatta's Neo-Café is famous for their masala dosais. Even celebrities from Bangalore come to taste it. On Sundays the waiting line is serpentine. It is somewhat like the Sears restaurant in San Francisco to which you took me one morning for their Swedish pancakes. We had to wait for such a long time in line before getting a table. All those wonderful experiences are still so fresh in my mind.

I had no appetite for breakfast as I told you. You were in Yalakki. You were bigger and better than breakfast. I was excited. I wanted to give you a great big hug. Even cry unashamedly. God had at last answered my night-and-day prayers. All things come to him who waits, I realised.

I horizontally prostrated myself before the deity in my temple for nearly fifteen minutes and repetitiously repeated my undying and eternal gratitude. I knew you were my ticket to freedom. How? I did not know. Frankly I did not care. Your very presence in Yalakki gave me hope and renewed strength. You would not have come if you did not have a plan to rescue me. You put me on top of the world. You made me feel like a million.

My immediate question was how to get in touch with you before my wife found you. If she did, then there would be no chance to talk to you at all. She would watch you like a hawk. Therefore, I had to find a means of getting in touch with you, but definitely not in the way I tried to do last time. I shuddered at the very thought of invading your privacy. Never again that route.

There was no time to waste. So I hastily scribbled a note: "Welcome to Yalakki. Must see you in complete privacy. Matter of life and death. Wait for further message from me." I signed it "Your loving son" and gave it to Subbu.

I commanded him not to breathe a word of the Robbed American Woman's arrival to that other woman. He knew who I meant.

"Swamiji, my lips are sealed," he replied and protested his loyalty to me, which was like my wife taking a vow of silence.

In less than half an hour Subbu returned and said that it was all a big mistake. It was an American man who had moved into the hotel. By bribing the hotel clerk two rupees (which I very much doubted because Subbu is as tightfisted as they come) he had been able to obtain the name of the American man. The name was scribbled on the same note on which I had written my message to you. He handed it to me. I deciphered the script. Horrors! to borrow the pregnant exclamation from Conrad's masterpiece, *Heart of Darkness*. It was Jeff.

Jeff Gleason, the arrogant brother of Virginia Gleason. I say arrogant, Mrs. Neilson, because Jeff, I was told, by none other than his own sister, got his kicks by imitating my un-American accent and reading out loud my private letters written to his sister. Thus he entertained his equally arrogant buddies, those sons and daughters of the California rich with their fast cars and faster drugs. Anyway, that is neither here nor there. I now had to cope with double disappointment: you not in Yalakki, first disappointment; Jeff Gleason in Yalakki, second disappointment, mixed with apprehension about what his actions would be.

The temperature of fear and anxiety increased. Why was Jeff in

Yalakki? What diabolical motive did he have? Puzzling questions that punctured my cloud nine and plummeted me to terra firma.

You see what I meant when I said I'm a yo-yo. Then it hit me! The reason for Jeff's arrival in Yalakki was "Secret Whispers," my private journal of philosophic reflections, poetry, and some fantasies! Virginia had written to me, a long time ago, that Jeff had removed (a very euphemistic word for "stolen") "Secret Whispers" without her permission. I had entrusted this precious volume of my private thoughts into her safekeeping.

I should have entrusted "Secret Whispers" to your care, Mrs. Neilson, the one trustworthy person in this whole wide world.

So here he was, Jeff that is, on my own turf, to further humiliate me. Was he planning to ascend the steps of the Cobra Temple in his tight and tattered blue jeans, dirty and stinking, and read out loud my private confessions? If my wife ever got a whisper of my "Secret Whispers," she would encourage Jeff to get in touch with that unscrupulous editor of *Blast*.

Mrs. Neilson, *Blast* is our version of the *National Enquirer*. Besides that, *Blast* is all headlines. In fact, it is often referred to as "Headlines Paper." Oh, yes, Mrs. Neilson, we have our tabloids too. Why not? Gossip is global, rumour is rampant.

While my mind was scripting scenarios and wrestling with Jeff Gleason's reasons for being in Yalakki and the possibilities of his forging an alliance with my wife and her cronies, we heard some footsteps, rather it was the slap, slap, flap, flap sound of broken sandals.

Subbu ran out, returned, and announced that it was Postmaster Gundappa.

That too caused considerable consternation. Why? I had been trying to get in touch with him, privately of course, but without success. Now he shows up.

Gundappa. The name literally means Round Father. But Gundappa is far from being round. He is all twigs and sticks, dry and brittle, a fragile skeleton of a man. He used to be a student of mine. He never completed his degree because he got married and had four children, one right after another. All of them girls, his karma. So he had to say good-bye to his educational aspirations and say welcome to human problems.

I am certain he knows who I am, behind this thick beard and this tentlike, saffron robe. Because I was his teacher and sent him two or three packets of used postage stamps from America, he plays the game and pretends he does not know me as his former teacher. I am grateful for that. He was an avid stamp collector then. I am not sure if he pursues this hobby now. I realise that the suffocating embrace of human problems can force out all interests in hobbies. Surviving from day to day becomes the chief hobby.

Gundappa bows to me and slowly folds himself to sit on the floor. I can almost hear the creak of his brittle bones.

"Coffee for Gundappa," I order Subbu.

Subbu gets busy to prepare a cup.

"Swamiji," says Gundappa and convulses with his dry, hoarse cough. "I have something to give you," he adds and goes into a slow, long-winded description of what it is, but without actually telling me what it is.

Subbu brings him a cup of coffee which further delays Gundappa's narration. He sips the coffee, praises Subbu's culinarian skills in the preparation of excellent coffee, blows on it, takes another sip, closes his eyes in sheer ecstasy, thanks me, and informs me of the hundreds and thousands of people pouring into Yalakki to witness my miracle in bringing forth rain on Sunday. He drinks some more coffee, asks Subbu for half a teaspoon of sugar, rests the coffee cup on the floor, and slowly stands up. He lifts up his dhoti and thrusts his right hand into the deep pocket of his thick khaki shorts, which reach well below his knees, and extracts a blue-and-red-bordered envelope.

The sight of the envelope excites me beyond description. I glimpse the colourful American postage stamps affixed to it. I know it is your letter. I eagerly stretch out my right hand to receive it.

Gundappa tucks the letter under his right arm and tightens the dhoti around his waist. Then he removes the letter from under his arm and slowly sits down with the letter on his lap and sips his coffee.

"Is that for me?" I ask him, trying to control my impatience. I know the letter is for me. I can see my name on it. But my name is typed, so it may not be from you. You have never typed letters to me.

Handwritten letters are more personal, has been your creed. Virginia always types her letters. So this letter could be from her, I realise with great sadness.

You see what I mean by saying I feel like a yo-yo. This constant up-and-down feeling within a matter of minutes and seconds.

There is no way you can rush Gundappa. He is like that. Even when he works in the post office, unless all his customers stand in a perfect line, one behind the other, he will not transact any kind of business.

So I simply sit back. Also as swamiji I had to maintain a detached attitude, an otherworld aura, the patience of a Job to borrow a biblical expression.

"Swamiji," Gundappa continued. "This letter arrived on January the fourth."

"January the fourth?" I ask.

"Yes. January the fourth. I tried and tried to somehow deliver this letter to you. But too many problems. Obstacles within obstacles. That woman, you know. . . ."

"Proceed," I interrupt, trying to speed his narration.

Gundappa has his own pace. It is slow, very, very slow. If I try to rush him, he will get flustered and retreat into silence and getting him to come out of that silent shell of sulking is as difficult as it is to slip in a word when my wife is speaking.

I describe this to you in detail so that you can comprehend my complex situation. Even getting a letter, transferring it from one hand to another, a simple natural process of communication, can take on the dimensions of a major drama. As a result I started to experience the trials and tribulations of an emotional roller coaster ride.

I again gestured Gundappa to continue.

He drank his coffee, draining it to the last drop, tapped the empty tumbler, and raised his finger to signal Subbu for another cup.

Subbu had squatted comfortably, eagerly watching the proceedings to report every minute detail to my wife. I looked at him sternly and he reluctantly got up to prepare another cup for Gundappa.

"Swamiji, every day that woman asking me, 'any letters from America?' Her eldest brother asking some questions too. My movements watched carefully by that woman's son Kittu. He has just become a scoundrel, so young and secretly smoking cigarettes. A pukka loafer. I explain all this to you, Swamiji, so you will know reason for the delay in the delivery of this letter."

Subbu brought another cup of coffee. Gundappa took a sip and frowned. He gestured that he needed some more sugar for his coffee. Subbu openly frowned at this demanding service and left to get him some sugar.

"Time for my prayers," I said as softly as I could, hoping that Gundappa would take a hint and hand over that letter.

"Swamiji, please continue your prayers and meditation," he said. "I can wait. Pray for me also, please. Due to some bureaucratic mismanagement I have not received my salary for two months. Two entire months, Swamiji. How can one survive? Family, children, relatives, so many obligations. So many mouths to feed. Instead of putting "G" they put "M." Simple spelling mistake resulting in matter of life and death. I was about to return check, properly registered, to the head office for correction of spelling and proper issuance of the check. But that woman's eldest brother said he could help. 'I have connections. I can take care of it. Just sign your name Mundappa instead of Gundappa. Put "M" instead of "G." I will get it cashed for a small commission. It will save you registered post amount and you can get money immediately in one or two days.' So like a simple and innocent fool. . . ."

At this point I got the message loud and clear. I knew why Gundappa was stalling. He needed his commission too to help him survive. So I raised my right hand to stop his anaconda. Ah, see, Mrs. Neilson, how I still remember you. Anaconda was one of the words I learned from you to describe someone who goes on and on and on, like my wife.

Anyway, I interrupted Gundappa and said: "Give me three numbers."

He responded immediately as though he had expected me to ask him that.

"Ten, twelve, twenty-one," he replied. He had come alive.

I closed my eyes, paused, and said, "Tomorrow, between nine and ten in the morning, go to the big well."

"Dry well? Suicide well?" he asked.

I nodded. "Behind one of the loose bricks," I said softly.

"Thank you, Swamiji," he said and bowed and handed me the letter.

He was about to rise.

I gestured him to stay. He sat down and held up his tumbler. Controlling his disgust, Subbu went to get him another cup of coffee. I hurriedly opened the envelope. There were four pages of a typed letter from Virginia and a note from you on your "From the Desk of Thelma Neilson" writing pad. Not a letter. Just a memo. A short note. Three sentences. Just three short simple sentences!

Such anticipation, such hope, such built-up expectations to hear from you for almost two to two and a half years. And now such a let-down! Such colossal disappointment. Oh, Mrs. Neilson, such a short note from you, like one of those homogenised 'have a happy day,' or 'get well soon,' or 'thank you, come again,' and so on and so forth mass-produced and mass-circulated statements sent to every Tom, Dick, and Harry in the United States. Frankly they are an affront to the rugged individualism preached with such passion in America.

So reading this three-short-simple-sentences memo from you is a terrific letdown, a down down, deep down letdown.

"My dear Raj, how are you? I think of you. Much love and affection. Thelma."

I read it several times. But that is all. Three sentences. No reference to my last letter. Not even the promise of a long letter. Nothing, nada. I try to bounce back up, on the upswing from those last four words. But I cannot. I just cannot get over the harsh reality of the shortness of your note. So short, so very short. Mrs. Neilson, I could just burst into tears.

At least it is something, I tried to console myself. Maybe you were busy with so many charitable things that you are always doing for your Lutheran church. Maybe Virginia appeared unannounced at your door when your hands were full packing clothing and food for starving children in Africa and Asia, and said: "Thelma, I'm about to drop a letter to Raj. You want me to say anything? Send him your love? If you want to scribble something real fast, I can stick it in this envelope before I lick it." Maybe, just maybe that might have happened. You therefore scribbled those three sentences. Not your fault, possibly Virginia's.

Whatever the circumstances, Mrs. Neilson, I need your help. I need your assistance to return to America, to Avalon.

I read Virginia's letter. It was mostly about her continuing state of spinsterhood and the various impediments to overcoming that status. The letter was full of Hamletian dilemmas concerning commitments and relationships and all that psychological claptrap which she picked up in those pop psychology courses she took so devotedly during the evenings. Poor Virginia, doomed to spinsterhood.

The letter was also full of information about her kid brother Jeff, who is supposed to be on this round-the-world trip, who might impulsively "just hike up to your neck of the woods." Well, he has. "If he does," she wrote "he'll personally give you 'Secret Whispers,'" and her fervent hope that he hasn't lost it and so on and so forth ad nauseam.

Absolutely nothing about me, not one word.

I hope Jeff does not run into my wife and casually hand over my journal. "This belongs to your husband. It's pretty good. You might enjoy reading it too. Could you give it to him. Say that Jeff returned it. Thanks loads." The very thought of that possibility sent ripples of fear down my spine. More anxiety. More yo-yo feeling.

"Good news?" Gundappa asked tentatively.

I casually folded the pages and thrust them back in the envelope and tossed it to a side.

"Too many demands for lecture tours," I said. "Americans simply hungry all the time for spiritual food," I added.

Gundappa's mouth opened in awe. He genuflected.

"Reply must go immediately. So many arrangements to be made," I said.

"Swamiji, I can wait for a reply. Then take it and personally post it," he offered.

"In two to three hours, reply will be ready," I said.

He tried to stand up.

"Gundappa," I said.

"Swamiji?"

"The American who has taken a room. . . ."

150

"Mr. Jeff Gleason?"

I nodded.

"Relative of . . ." he pointed to the return address on the envelope.

"Brother," I said.

"Oh," he said with surprise, followed by an "ah" of enlightenment. "He has personally come to take you," he said, midway between a statement and a question.

Inadvertently Gundappa had provided me with a possibility. Why not? I said to myself. Desperate situations need desperate remedies. Did not Winston Churchill say: "If it'll help England I'll shake hands with the devil"?

I put my finger to my lips to signal Gundappa that the matter is very hush-hush.

Gundappa nodded deferentially, privileged to be a part of this confidentiality. Subbu returned with a fresh pot of coffee and filled Gundappa's empty tumbler. He added some milk and announced: "Sugar exhausted."

"Coffee without sugar?" Gundappa said, his face recomposing itself into a bitter frown.

Subbu wanted to squat on his haunches and listen to the conversation. He sensed both gossip and conspiracy, a heady combination he could not resist.

I stopped him halfway down.

"Moorthy's mansion," I said.

"Now?" he asked.

"Important message," I emphasised.

"Very, very hot, Swamiji," he pleaded, waving his hands expansively towards the shimmering heat outside.

"If you wish to go to America . . ." I started, letting the words dangle like an unspoken promise. I glanced at the red-and-blue-bordered envelope. He stood up and became alert.

"Subbu?" Gundappa inquired with wide-eyed astonishment at the possibility of this barefoot boy, round and plump, going to America where the streets are paved with gold and the trees sprout dollar bills.

Subbu grinned with superiority.

"All in God's hands," I said. Gundappa read my eyes asking him to be silent.

151

He blew on the hot tumbler of coffee and sipped, the bitterness reflected in his face.

"Tell Mani to see me in private. Most important," I said to Subbu. Subbu left. "Do you want to use some jaggery to sweeten the coffee?" I asked Gundappa.

For your information, Mrs. Neilson, jaggery is pure sugarcane juice unrefined and condensed into either big or small cubes. They have the colour of maple syrup which I used to enjoy while I was in Avalon.

"Jaggery in coffee?" Gundappa asked with unconcealed disgust. Then he started to praise me for my fame and fortune and what a privilege it was for him to have known me. I interrupted his praise.

"Two things I need from you," I said.

"I am at your service," he said.

"I have to reply to this letter. You must post it promptly," I said.

"Swamiji, I have already promised to do that."

"You have to deliver a message to Jeff Gleason. . . ."

"Not to worry. It will be delivered personally with utmost secret confidentiality," he interrupted me.

I quickly wrote a brief note: "Jeff, welcome to Yalakki. It is of utmost importance that I meet you in complete privacy. Mani will arrange our meeting. Confidentiality is crucial. Matter of life and death." I underlined confidentiality and signed it Raj and handed it to Gundappa.

He concealed it in his thick khaki shorts. I asked him to return after he had delivered my message to Jeff by which time I would have completed my letter to you.

He said that would be too much exhaustion because of the heat and that he would wait, possibly even take a nap, while I completed the letter.

I agreed with him and have wasted no time in writing and completing this letter to you. I have reported everything to you. That is the only way by which I can give you a correct picture of the state of my body and mind.

I will enlist Jeff's assistance to help me escape from this self-imprisonment. How this help will shape up, I do not know. But I must leave Yalakki and reach Bangalore before the fatal hour of high noon on Sunday, two days from today.

Once I reach Bangalore, I have to rely on your help to reach Avalon.

Hope has surged. I feel upbeat. Short as your letter is, at least you remember me. You think of me. Frivolous and arrogant as Jeff might be, he is here. A visible human link from Avalon. What was it you always used to say, turn disadvantage into advantage; weakness into strength. That is what I will attempt to do.

So there it is, Mrs. Neilson. Here I stand, ready to take the leap.

Your loving son,

Raj

2

My dearest Mrs. Neilson:

This is your old and dearest friend Vimala writing about important matters.

What an astonishment I had only some time ago.

I just could not believe it. I pinched myself to make certain that I was not dreaming. Last night I really did dream that I was sitting in your kitchen in America and putting "From the private kitchen of Vimala" labels on the bottles. Remember how you ordered those labels for me? That is how you got me started on my private business. We'll make you a capitalist, Vimala, you said, helping me to sell pickles, papadams, and other assorted condiments to your friends in the Avalon branch of the American Business and Professional Women's Association.

You will be glad to know that I have sincerely followed your suggestions. You are truly my inspiration in this private business attempt—which has expanded. Not too much but enough to keep our body and soul alive, mine and my son Kittu's. It has not been an easy business. Because of the severe drought we are facing, it is very difficult to buy proper lemons and mangoes. Most of them have very little juice in them. I have much more demand than I can supply. Added

153

to this my eldest brother is regularly asking me to supply his new hotel with my pickles.

Yes, Mrs. Neilson, my eldest brother now has a rip-roaring tourist hotel business in Bangalore. The tourist hotel is called Peacock Paradise, since peacock is the national bird of our country. The tourist hotel is cent percent Western style.

I must also tell you that my eldest brother is hoping to attend an international tourist conference in California, close to Disneyland. He is trying hard to be selected as one of the delegates from India, so he can get foreign exchange. I have already given him your address so he can meet you and pay his respects. I will send some fresh lemon pickles with him as a small token of my appreciation. Foreign exchange is a serious problem. Therefore I cannot come with my eldest brother to America and give him some useful tips on adjusting to American life. I hope he will be selected as a delegate. But there is so much dirty politics, and big government officials are always pushing their relatives even if they do not have any qualifications.

If you don't mind and if it is not too much trouble, could you ask one of the important persons organising the tourist conference to write a letter to my eldest brother inviting him to the conference. The letter must say, We have heard of the famous Peacock Paradise Hotel which is contributing so much towards world tourism. That will impress the foreign exchange people here to permit my brother to travel. There is a little slip of paper enclosed with his name and address.

You may remember, Mrs. Neilson, that when I was in Avalon I tried so hard to convince my husband to invest money and purchase a refrigerator. But do you think he listened to me? No. He simply wasted his money on cigarettes and other fleeting pleasures of the body. If he had purchased an American-type refrigerator, my eldest brother and myself could have simply made enormous amounts of money both in the tourist hotel business and in my private business. It was a golden opportunity lost. He is always like that, my husband, missing golden opportunities one after another. When opportunity knocks on his door, it is always locked.

The only way to supply eldest brother's hotel needs is to use inferior dry lemons and wrinkled mangoes. That I will not do. Why? It is simple answer. Remember what you once told me, Mrs. Neilson?

Vimala, you said, There are three parts to quality. Part one is quality; part two is quality; and part three is quality. I remember that like it was yesterday. So I will not substitute quantity for quality. You continue to be my inspiration even though oceans separate us.

Sorry to get away from the main topic but I have so much to tell you. Last night I dreamed of you, but then this afternoon about two to three hours ago I am sitting in my house, on the veranda, and filling bottles with lemon pickles. My husband, your dear Raj, is still leading a double life, Swamiji by day and Romeo by night. He has become the Hyde and Jekyll of Yalakki. So I have to be the breadwinner of the house. Making pickles, etc., etc. Selling them, earning a little money, praying to God to grant my husband some intelligence so he can return to normal life, taking care of his household responsibilities, being a husband to his wife and a father to his son. So doing a little business just to survive and praying to the Almighty God for granting sanity to my husband is my entire life these days.

My mother-in-law, my husband's own mother, passed away while staying with her daughter in Kolar. Mrs. Neilson, it is very sad for me to report that my husband did not even go to Kolar to attend her funeral. Eldest son, according to our Hindu traditions, must perform the sacred rituals to ensure the proper satisfaction of the soul in its flight from the body. I simply shed tears like a river for my mother-in-law's sad fate in not having her eldest son perform these rituals.

Kittu and I took the night train and went to Kolar for the ceremonies. I also took bottles of pickles as gifts for my sister-in-law. But she never even treated me with proper respect and openly said that my pickles were very salty. That is a big story which I will tell you some other time but you must excuse me for not telling it to you this time.

I returned from Kolar and went to see my husband, and I managed to let him know that I had gone to visit the death of his mother. I thought he would shed tears, even crocodile tears for the sake of appearance. But do you know what he did? He said, Death is a natural state of life, like birth. Life is *maya*. Maya means illusion. I felt so angry and wanted to say openly, What kind of a son are you not even shedding one drop of tear for the woman who carried you for nine months in her womb and brought you into this life? But out of respect for dignity I simply controlled myself.

155

Last time I wrote you I clearly told you how my husband had returned to Yalakki and moved into the Cobra Temple and proclaimed himself Swamiji of Yalakki. I also told you how it was my husband who scared you in your hotel room. I hope you have received that letter and digested all the facts I presented to you.

Then I never heard from you. Not complaining, Mrs. Neilson. I know how busy you are, always doing this or doing that.

Then suddenly last night I dreamed of you. So today I said to myself that if you have come in my dream you must be thinking of me. I made up my mind to write you a letter. I have never forgotten you. Even my son Kittu still remembers the tasty chocolates you gave him many years ago.

That is why when my neighbour Seetha came to me about two to three hours ago and said, Robbed American Woman has come back and taken room in New Modern Hotel, I could not believe that news. Yalakki people out of pure affection have given you that nickname as Robbed American Woman.

Robbed American Woman? Are you sure? I asked Seetha.

Yes, she said. Beggar boy Subbu told me. Then she explained that she had met Subbu, who was running so fast he just dashed into her. By way of explaining why he was in such a hurry, he explained that he was hurrying to see the swamiji to give him the news of your arrival. Then he requested Seetha to keep the matter to herself and not tell anyone. But Seetha is known for spreading news both true and false. She has equal respect for both. Tell Seetha something and say don't tell it to anyone, it is a guarantee that it will spread like wildfire. Anyway, she told me of your arrival and said, You must go and welcome her because you know her and you have been in America. She also wanted to stay and gossip, but I have no time for gossip. As I told you my time is devoted to business and prayer.

After Seetha gave me the news, I stopped my bottle-pickling work and walked over to the New Modern Hotel to meet you.

The hotel office, which is really a small table, three chairs, and an electric fan, was deserted. There was a sign on the desk saying No Vacancy. Typical case of rats will play when cat is away. Owner is away in Singapore so employees take holiday! Also, Mrs. Neilson, that sign outside the hotel saying Reasonable Rates with the letter E

missing is still the same. So it still reads Reasonable Rat s. I remember
how you laughed and took a picture of the sign to show your girl-
friends. Please do not show that picture at the tourist conference!

I simply walked through the corridor and reached the back porch
and waited. I am sure you remember this porch because it is in one of
the rooms around this porch that you stayed. Room number seven. I
remember it so clearly. Since nothing comes to him who simply waits,
I took the bold step of knocking on the rooms to see in which one you
were staying. First three rooms, knock, no answer. Fourth one, I hit
jackpot as you Americans say.

Who is it? American man's voice. Not woman's. The door opens
a little bit. I see American man, only wearing red-coloured underwear.
He sees me. Wait, he says and closes door.

Sorry to disturb you, Sir. Sir, I am looking for Mrs. Thelma
Neilson, I say.

After a few minutes, the door opens again. The man is now
wearing blue jeans with shirt. He is yawning. Oh, is it coffee time
already? he asks.

I'm looking for Mrs. Thelma Neilson, I again say.

Is she here? he asked.

Yes, because that is what my friend told me, I reply.

Thelma Neilson? Oh, no, he says, and says something about tasty
shoes which I do not understand.

Shoes? I ask.

Never mind. Is she really here? he asks.

Yes, I just found out, I say.

Hey, wait a second, he says, coming out of the room. I know
you. You were in Avalon. You're Raj's wife. Right?

Yes. I have also seen you.

I'm Jeff. Jeff Gleason, Ginny's brother, he says and reaches out
his hand for a handshake, then pulls it back and greets me with folded
hands. *Namaste*, he says.

Namaste is North Indian. *Namaskara* is South Indian, I say.

OK, whichever, whatever, he says. For a second I thought you
were from the hotel with my afternoon coffee. Sorry, he says and
laughs.

Where is Mrs. Neilson? I ask.

Search me, he says.

Why should I search you? That is job of police, I say.

It's an expression. Never mind. I don't know where Mrs. Neilson is.

Anyway, Mrs. Neilson, he says one thing, I say something. Total confusion, total misunderstanding. One thing definite, *you* are not in Yalakki. Big disappointment for me, for my son Kittu. But this Jeff is in Yalakki. Why him? He says he just came. Just like that, no reason. That is a big lie. Why would anyone come to this little town? What is there for an American to see? He is not fooling me. Took bus and just came, he says to me. Who is he kidding? He is here, sent by his sister, that Virginia Gleason, to help my husband escape. But this Jeff does not know that my husband is in tighter than a prison in that Cobra Temple. I tell him that. I have nothing to hide. I am very honest, you know that, Mrs. Neilson.

We stand and stare, this Jeff and I.

At this time, Mrs. Neilson, this Mr. Money Mani arrives. He is very fat, roly-poly you can say. This Mr. Money Mani is Saroja's husband. Do you remember Saroja? Only to refresh your memory, let me tell you that Saroja has been the secret sweetheart of my husband. Not so secret because it is an open secret. That is a well-known fact.

I cannot remember whether I told you or not in my last letter, how I used to cook my husband's favorite foods, just the way he liked them, and take them devotedly to his abode in the Cobra Temple. After all, bogus or nonbogus, a husband is a sacred person to an Indian wife.

Mrs. Neilson, you know that I have been to America. I can speak and write like any other American woman, although with my own Indian style. I am also a professional businesswoman with my own pickle business, but deep inside within me I am a cent percent woman of Indian culture and ancient philosophy.

Then one day my husband dismisses me. Just like that. You don't have to bring me any more food, he says. Special food prepared by Udipi cook will be sent in a car from Moorthy's Mansion. I agree that Udipi cooks are famous, but is that the way for a husband to treat his wife? You tell me. Then he tells me that his fame has spread and that Moorthy and his son-in-law Mani want him to help them. How will you help them? I ask. He tells me that Moorthy and Mani want him to perform some magic so that barren-wombed Saroja can have a child.

Now, Mrs. Neilson, I must tell you that this roly-poly Mani cannot make Saroja pregnant even if he stands on the top of his head. Why? The answer is simple. Mani likes boys. That is no rumour. It is the truth. Of course I have nothing against that. Love is love.

Now Saroja is a little pregnant. By that I mean not too much of stomach pushed forward although she is very close to nine months.

But how can she be pregnant if roly-poly Mani cannot give her the necessary push? That is the one-hundred-thousand-dollar question.

Swamiji is claiming that he is responsible because of his spiritual powers. That is humbug. He is responsible, no doubt, but not by spiritual powers. Swamiji made Saroja pregnant same way any man makes a woman pregnant. Mrs. Neilson, you must forgive me for being so direct. I cannot tell it any other way.

Saroja going to Cobra Temple in the middle of the night. Bogus swamiji going to Moorthy Mansion in special car. Poojas, prayers, prostrations, performances, etc., etc. Behind all this mumbo jumbo, a lot of hanky-panky. Suddenly, barren Saroja gets a little stomach push. These ignorant, stupid, superstitious people of Yalakki actually believe that Swamiji said prayers, sprinkled holy Ganges water, and made Saroja pregnant. His fame and reputation increase.

Mani floats on the ocean of joy because with one stroke, Swamiji turns Money Mani into a macho man and Saroja has stomach push. The real truth behind all this I know, Saroja knows, Mani knows, and now you know.

Therefore, Mrs. Neilson, how can I allow this bogus swamiji to escape from Yalakki?

I will expose him on Sunday, two days from today. Thousands have come, and thousands more will come to see him bring forth rain from the heavens. He has promised that miracle. Real holy men are praying all over India for rain. Not a drop. How can bogus swamiji produce rain? He can produce a baby behind prayer curtain, but rain? No way, San Jose.

Anyway, to go back to what I was saying, this Mani rolling in wealth his ancestors made out of corrupt methods arrives while Jeff and I are talking.

Mani folds his baby-fat pudgy palms, smiles, and bows to Jeff. Jeff bows back.

Sorry for the interruption. But could you be Mr. Jeff Gleason from the golden state of California? he asks.

Guilty as charged, Jeff says.

No, no. Not guilty, you are our honoured guest. My name is Mani, short for a long name. Welcome to Yalakki, Mani says.

Thank you. You two know each other?

Mani smiles and nods. He has more gold in his mouth than I have in my bangles.

Mrs. Neilson, I return home very sad because you are not in Yalakki as I was told. How can someone mistake Jeff for you? That is the nature of this small town. Someone says one thing and by the time it reaches someone else, the news is totally different. It is because of this that a bogus swamiji can thrive in this town and make so many people believe him to be a miracle man. You know what happened in your own case. My husband broke into your room. But the incident has taken on so many different stories. The fact that a hundred dollars had been stolen from your room spread like wildfire. There were some people who even consulted my husband to find out where the stolen money was hidden. I don't know what answer he gave or did not give. Because I don't know, I am not going to say whether it is true or false. Some say that the swamiji located the hundred dollars and kept half for himself. True or false? I do not know. Because I don't know, I'm not going to say if it is true or false. That is because I am basically an honest person.

Mrs. Neilson, I have much work to do. I have to work to keep my business. I have to work to see that my husband does not escape. Therefore I will end this letter now.

I have one request for you. Please keep out of our business.

This is like civil war between my husband and me. So keep away. Just eat your McDonald hamburgers and drink Coca-Cola and let me take care of this bogus swamiji of Yalakki. But don't forget to have the tourist conference organiser write my eldest brother who is proprietor of the famous Peacock Paradise Hotel to invite him to the tourist conference near Disneyland.

Your sincere friend,
Vimala

3

My dear Mother Neilson:

I hope and pray that my earlier letter is winging its way to you as fast as possible.

Your recent letter sent through Virginia through her brother Jeff, who by the way arrived safely in Yalakki, was most welcome and gratefully appreciated. I apologise for having accused you in my previous letter, the winging-its-way letter just mentioned, for the three-short-sentences brevity of your communication. Your most recent letter has infused new hope, new vitality, and that feeling of Robert Browningian robust optimism toward life.

Before I go any further, let me express to you my deepest and heartfelt condolences on the loss of your closest friend, Mary Gerber. I can very well understand your loneliness and that dreadful feeling of being at loose ends. Even though surrounded by crowds, I feel utterly lonely and I too am at loose ends. The news about my alma mater Avalon College on the verge of closing its doors of learning brought tears to my eyes. Fallen upon evil days and evil tongues, as John Milton said. But I shall never ever forget the glorious days of my study within its hallowed halls. And of course, without a doubt, meeting you and developing this lifelong son-mother relationship is like the Jewel in the Crown of my Avalon experience.

But, Mrs. Neilson, the question is, what next? I have shed my tears. You have shed yours. What now? You have told me to go to Madras and contact the American consul there. He is the nephew of a friend of yours. Yes. Yes. I want to but I am bound to this rock like Prometheus. And if I get there, what do I say?

I have a thought. It is actually your idea. I will merely expand on it. Let me humbly suggest what I think will be the Phoenix rising out of the ashes. You have mentioned my doing something creative with the now defunct Avalon College. Yoga, Indian culture, and so on. Why not start a meditation center? We can call it Avalon Ashram, a place of peace and tranquility where people can come to heal their hearts and minds. Avalon College can have a new birth. A new reincarnation. You and I can work as a team. It will be our contribution to this weary world. Perhaps your American consul nephew is a man of vision.

Oh, how exciting this thought is. I wish I were there right now, so we could start toward creating Avalon Ashram. My need to get out of Yalakki takes on a new sense of urgency, a nobler purpose.

Now, back to the immediate matter at hand. I met Jeff. I have to give credit where credit is due and want to change my former opinion of him as an irresponsible young man. He has matured remarkably. He still retains that unique American passion for the pursuit of happiness. But his travels around the world have added a touch of seriousness, which has resulted in his gaining that refreshingly welcome quality of maturity.

He returned my journal and complimented me on its literary quality and thought that Vanity Press might publish it. Do you know this press? I wish to get their address and explore possible publication. Mrs. Neilson, after editing the book properly, I wish to dedicate "Secret Whispers" to you, if I can get it published. We will discuss this when we meet in Avalon. I will, however, not accept no for an answer. On the matter of dedication, I am firm.

Jeff is very creative and innovative and has outlined a possible plan for my escape from Yalakki en route to America to be your partner in bringing forth AA from AC. You know what I mean.

Saroja's elderly aunt has arrived from the town of Bellary to assist with the birth of the baby. She is in her eighties, give or take a year or two. No one, particularly of her generation, keeps exact birth dates. For all we know she may be 90. But she is a tough cookie. Grey-haired, but with plenty of it, she is about my height and rather on the plump side. She has a round, serene face, though with quite a bit of facial hair, which gives her a masculine countenance. She is definitely a no-nonsense type, quite independent, and is like a mother to motherless Saroja. This mother cum aunt or vice versa, who has over these many years prayed to more gods and goddesses than there are in the Hindu pantheon, is overjoyed that at last Saroja is giving birth to a baby.

Auntie's belief is that it is my magical, spiritual, call it what you will, power which has resulted in this miracle. Now, there are a lot of rumours concerning Saroja's pregnancy. Yalakki being a small town, rumours and gossip are part of the very air you breathe. It is this town's own homegrown soap opera, if you will. Of course my wife actively fuels these rumours and in the process maligns innocent people. Her wild and weird imagination makes her believe that something illicit has happened between me and Saroja, resulting in her pregnancy. As mentioned earlier, in my youth there might have been a romantic desire for Saroja. But it was one of those "loved and lost and never to have loved again" situations.

Anyway, let me not dwell on these gossips and rumours and unnecessarily dignify them.

Back to the immediate matter at hand. I met Jeff in Mani's mansion. That itself is an accomplishment. Saroja is expecting delivery of her child within a matter of days. For this important event I was asked to be present by both Saroja and her husband Mani. They wanted my presence so that I could pray and chant the proper verses and proper syllables to assure an auspicious atmosphere to usher in their eagerly awaited first child. So Mani sent his good car—a 1978 Oldsmobile in tip-top condition—along with his driver to have me transported to their home.

Of course, the moment the car pulled up in front of the Cobra Temple and the second I emerged from the temple to get into the car, my wife's army of agents positioned themselves strategically to watch me. I was certain that my wife and her eldest brother had also stationed clandestine agents on the road leading to Bangalore so that they could stop me if ever I tried to make a getaway. To Jeff I confessed the truth, the whole truth, and nothing but the truth: "I must escape from Yalakki. I must get to Bangalore. You must help me. I need you." These were my simple but direct words.

"I'm sure we can work something out," he said. When Auntie personally served coffee for me and Jeff, he observed her very closely and seemed to study both of us. "Perfect," he murmured. "I've got it," he said in the tone and manner of the Greek philosopher who got out of his bathtub naked saying, "Eureka!"

"Got what?" I asked.

"The answer. The first thing we have to do is spread the word among everyone in Yalakki, particularly to your wife and her brother, that Auntie is here, that she's not well. She's old and in frail health. Her heart is weak and the long bus trip and the heat have aggravated her condition."

"Mr. Jeff, not to worry on that," Mani said. "Everyone already knows Auntie's here. Everyone also knows that Auntie's here in connection with my wife's expected baby. This is a small town. News spreads fast. In fact, I am told by my cook that Vimala has already made enquiries about whether Auntie had actually arrived, how long she would be staying, etc., etc. As for Auntie's ill health, that is a natural state of her being. Ill health and elderly age go together. It is natural to be suffering from aches and pains, colds and coughs, shortness of breath and weakness of heart, diarrhea, and other assorted bodily frailties."

"OK," Jeff said. "Here's what we'll do. Let's see if we can pull off a switch."

"Switch?" I asked.

"Yes. We'll dress Auntie up to look like you and you up like Auntie and then. . . ."

"What?" I was stupefied by the suggestion. "Me dress up . . . ?"

"Sure. Why not?"

"But I don't look like Auntie! My beard, my body—I am stouter, and. . . ."

"No problem. We can work it out. Did you ever see Jack Lemmon and Tony Curtis in. . . ."

"*Some Like It Hot*," I said right away. "Oh, how thoroughly I enjoyed that movie in America."

But the idea seemed farfetched, until Jeff started describing it in detail. Then I was amazed how this young man's mind worked. He was definitely a take-charge type.

"Hey, this is fun," he said, as we got down to nailing in the brass tacks. "We'll call it 'Operation Holy Heist.' Maybe we can sell the rights to Mel Brooks. I can see it on the marquee—'*The Holy Heist*, starring Gene Wilder and Cleavon Little.' Can't you see Madeline Kahn playing Vimala!"

Then he outlined the plan like a seasoned military general. I congratulated him on his organising abilities and told him that he ought to have been in the military. He said he hated the military and attributed his superb organising skills to his leadership and experiences in planning fraternity pranks in college. However or wherever he learned it, I earnestly hope and devoutly pray that it works.

The plan is for Auntie, dressed as me, to ride to Cobra Temple in Mani's old car to distract the crowd and draw Vimala's agents. I, dressed as Auntie, will start to follow in the new car, but will have a sudden heart attack and be rushed off to Bangalore—and freedom!

"Timing is the key," Jeff said as he gave us our instructions. He even made us, that is, Auntie and myself and the drivers of the cars, go through a sort of rehearsal: who gets into which car, who gets out first at the Cobra Temple, etc. I will not go into all those details because of lack of time.

So, Mrs. Neilson, the stage is set on which I'm going to play my biggest role, exchanging my dhoti for a sari. Quite frankly, I wish I didn't have to do it this way. I'm rather nervous. What if the whole thing falls apart at the last minute, etc., etc.? Jeff keeps saying I should relax and play it cool. "Be natural, go for it. Break a leg," he keeps repeating. I certainly hope and pray that it will not be literal, this break a leg.

Jeff has got his camera all set to take my picture looking like respectable old Auntie. "Raj, we'll be laughing about all this once it's over and you're out of this trap," he keeps saying.

Mrs. Neilson, assuming Jeff's plan works and I'm out, what will happen when the crowd finds out the truth? I have this terrible feeling that I am not doing the right thing. That I am running away like a coward, disappointing all those thousands who believe in me. What a lot of responsibility I've taken on, even though it was thrust upon me.

Mrs. Neilson, I am truly in the throes of a dilemma. Escaping from my wife, that is a joyous prospect. Coming to work with you, that is a noble cause. Escaping or rather fleeing from my devotees, that part hurts me, makes me feel shameful. But I have sincerely vowed to myself to make it up to them. Somehow, by hook or crook, I shall make it up to them. I pledged to do something unselfishly good for all these people who have honored me by acknowledging me with total sincerity as their beloved Guruji. Working for AA will exonerate me. My mea culpa.

While my mind was a simmering, steaming cauldron of conflicting thoughts, Jeff urged me to bite the bullet and do what has to be done.

"Gotta give it your all," Jeff urged.

So, Mrs. Neilson, I will give it my all. I hope I am doing the right thing. I wish there were a better way, or should I say a more honourable way, to exit from Yalakki. But Jeff has gone to all this trouble. So has Mani and Auntie and, of course, you, over there, thousands of miles away ready to welcome me so we can build our Avalon Ashram for the good of mankind. I cannot let all of you down. I must go through with it, go through with Operation Holy Heist.

I am sending this letter, possibly my last before I see you, in the same envelope Jeff has addressed to Ginny. I hope that as soon as Ginny gets her brother's letter, she'll remove my letter and deliver it to you posthaste. I know she will.

Mrs. Neilson, see you soon. I hope. I pray.

Your affectionate son,
Raj

4

Dear Ginny,

This is your ne'er-do-well brother reporting in. I'm writing from the South Indian hill resort of Ootacamund, Ooty for short. I left Yalakki a few days ago, spent a couple of days in Bangalore, and then took the bus to Ooty. What a welcome change from the blistering heat of the plains. Ooty used to be a British hill station during the reign of the Pukka Sahib. It's about 7,000 feet above sea level in the celebrated Blue Hills of South India. The gently rolling landscape and buildings with Victorian gables make me think of the English country-side. My plan to fly out of Bombay next week to New York and on to San Francisco has changed. As long as I'm in India, I might as well see as much of this country as possible. So it looks like I'll be bumming around for a bit longer.

Things happened fast and furious after my recent letter to you. Remember in the last episode Raj had been tricked by Vimala into guaranteeing to bring rain to end the drought and was desperate to get away before the fateful hour he had predicted came (which was last Sunday afternoon). Well, Raj escaped from Yalakki, but it was touch and go. He almost didn't make it.

We called it Operation Holy Heist (clever, huh?). I won't go into excruciating detail. I gather Raj described the plan in his letter to goody-two-shoes Thelma and you've probably already gotten it from her. It involved a role switch in which Raj dressed up as Auntie and vice versa. At the right moment he (as Auntie) would have a heart attack and be rushed off to the hospital in Bangalore, while she (as Raj) fended off the crowd. We'd given it a dry run at Mani's house (mansion actually), hidden behind the walls that surround it—the two cars, Raj and Auntie made up as each other, the fake heart attack, a thorough briefing on who'd do what at what time, every detail—and it looked like it would work.

Raj was hilarious in his white sari with some of that spongy styrofoam from my camera bag (it protects the telephoto lens) stuffed in the bra for breasts and the sash wrapped around his face to hide his beard. I began to wonder if we could pull it off until he got in the car where the view of him was sufficiently obscured to enable him to pass. I took some photos of him which seemed to annoy him no end.

Auntie looked just as funny. We made up some whiskers from the shorn hair of the devotees. People visiting the Cobra Temple will often make pledges (I was told) to have their heads shaved if they get their wishes. I understand that quite a bit of this hair, women's in particular, is shipped overseas for fancy wigs. Anyway, I sent one of Mani's servants to salvage some hair for Auntie's makeup. We managed to get them stuck to her face, but she looked more like something from outer space than an Indian holy man. We heaped the robes on, however, so that inside the car she looked okay. But once she stepped out, that crowd would have to be pretty gullible not to catch on immediately.

Then, right in the middle of everything, Saroja went into labor. Panic! This should not happen, Mani kept babbling, because the local astrologer had predicted that the baby (which he said would be a boy) would not arrive for another ten days. Before Saroja could be rushed to the hospital in Bangalore, she had her baby (totally disregarding the astrologer). Mani, who is fat and all flab and sickeningly polite and sweet (when he speaks he sounds like an Indian Liberace), left the scene. Auntie is amazing. She shooed everyone away except a couple of other women and took charge as midwife par excellence! I could hear her giving orders, and people hurried about getting hot water and towels and other things I couldn't identify until finally you could hear the baby crying and Auntie came out with a worried look on her face.

She, Raj, and Mani huddled for a few minutes, talking rapidly. I wondered if something was wrong with Saroja. Despite being pregnant, she'd seemed very small and frail. Her baby must have been tiny, but I didn't see it. Finally, Raj came over to me with a solemn face and I really got worried.

"Is something wrong?"

"No, though Auntie is a little concerned about Saroja. She's quite weak."

I wanted to congratulate Mani, but I had seen him hurriedly leave the room, obviously upset.

"What's the matter with Mani?" I asked Raj.

"The baby's a girl. He was hoping for a boy, who'd be an heir to his name and fortune. In India boys are preferred, particularly the firstborn," Raj explained. "He thinks that if only Saroja had delayed giving birth for another ten days, it'd have been a boy, just as the astrologer prophesied." I guess Mani doesn't know much about the birds and the bees.

It was pretty gloomy around there until Auntie finished tending to Saroja. Then she came out and said something that Raj translated as "Let's continue this show on the road."

She was still all fired up and ready to go, but Raj was having second thoughts. He kept asking Auntie over and over again, "What'll you do when they find out who you are?" At first she told him patiently not to worry about her, that she'd take care of herself. After all she was eighty years old, what difference did it make—that seemed to be her attitude. But Raj kept after her about it until she finally, in effect, told him to go soak his head. I don't know, but I'm pretty sure Raj got cold feet. I almost got the feeling toward the end that he wanted it to fail. He wanted to be exposed and to face the consequences.

The original plan was for Raj, who stayed with us at Mani's until it was time to go, to leave in the Oldsmobile, the one in tip-top condition, dressed as Auntie, feigning a heart attack and being driven off to a hospital in Bangalore. In the other car, the worn-out, one-workable-door Ford, of uncertain vintage, Auntie dressed as Raj would head for the Cobra Temple. All they had to do was fool Vimala's agents ("my wife's KGB," Raj called them) who were posted outside Mani's in the crowd that was always hanging around waiting to get a look at their swamiji.

But Mani's father-in-law sent word that the tip-top Oldsmobile be sent to Bangalore to chauffeur a VIP from Delhi. Mani had to follow orders. So we were stuck with the Ford. Plans were changed to take both Raj and Auntie in one car. Mani said that if he had time, he could get another car from Bangalore, since he had connections. "All it requires is for an announcement to be made from the Cobra Temple that Guruji requires more time for his prayers."

"It's OK by me," I said, but Raj wouldn't hear of it. "We proceed according to schedule," he said grimly. "My devotees are awaiting their Guruji." It seemed a little weird for him to be worrying about his devotees when he was in the process of bugging out on them, but as I said, his mental state wasn't A-1 at this point. Even his conversation reflected his tension. "We take a chance. Use one car. Auntie sit in front seat, I sit in back seat. Moment Auntie steps out, I pretend heart attack and car will rush me through crowd and drive fast to Bangalore."

"OK," I said, "but once you get to the temple, I'm not sure you'll get out. The place is jammed and. . . ."

"Not to mind," he replied. "As you Americans say, it is my funeral." He seemed totally resigned to whatever fate had in store for him.

Mani sent one of his servants ahead to announce that Guruji was on his way and to try to clear a path for the car. I wished Raj good luck and left with the servant. A large crowd had gathered around Moorthy's mansion to watch the Guruji depart. I tried to spot Vimala's agents but found that everyone seemed to look alike.

My main problem now was the heat. You cannot imagine how hot it was. I've never experienced anything like it. Just in the short walk to Cobra Temple I was totally drenched in sweat. All I could think of was the old song, "Only mad dogs and Englishmen go out in the noonday sun."

The area around the temple was packed and people were still streaming in. It was like a scene from that Gandhi movie—a sea of brown bodies in white loincloths or saris stretching in every direction. "Boy, this is India," was all I could think. But there was no way a car was going to get in and out of that mass of humanity quickly. Once in, it would simply be absorbed by the zillions of bodies. At one edge I found a dry mound of earth which was unoccupied, apparently because you couldn't see the temple entrance from it. But it put me near the route the car would take and gave me a good view of its approach. I was unable to spot Vimala or her brother, though I knew they were there, possibly out of my line of sight, close to the temple.

A little while later I saw Mani's car slowly moving toward the area. Others spotted it too. A surge of excitement swept through the crowd. The frenzied chanting began, "Guruji, Guruji."

A slim young man managed to climb the mound of earth beside me, precariously balancing himself and clutching my waist. He apologized and introduced himself as a newspaper reporter.

"I am Sharma. And you are?"

I told him and, reporter that he was, he wanted to know all about me and my *real* reason for being in this small town to witness this "about-to-take-place miracle." I got what he was hinting at, so I lowered my voice to a proper conspiratorial whisper and said, "Sharma, I'll be honest with you. I can't be otherwise in the vicinity of this holy place. I'm working as a free-lancer for the CIA."

170

"I knew it. I knew it," Sharma enthused and would have fallen off the mound if I hadn't steadied him.

"Let's talk, later," I said.

"Certainly, certainly," he said. "I particularly want to discuss the role of morality and immorality in American foreign policy."

"That's my special area of expertise," I said.

As the car approached, the crowd's excitement increased. They made no effort to part and let the car through. It almost looked as if they were trying to block it. Several people attempted to prostrate themselves, but there was no room and a couple almost got trampled. As the car came into view they all raised their hands, palms joined in respectful salutation.

Actually, it was an awesome sight, and I'd have been very impressed if I hadn't been so sure the whole thing was going to come to a disastrous end. Operation Holy Heist was beginning to look a bit crackbrained.

The car was slowed to a crawl by the people around it and finally came to a halt near where I was perched. The driver got out, hoping to clear a path, but the crowd surged forward and surrounded the car. Raj, dressed as Auntie, was sitting in the backseat. I tried to catch his eye, but he was leaning forward talking to Auntie. Then I noticed something strange going on with Auntie in the front seat. She was shaking her head back and forth and pulling at her robe. I jumped up and waded through the crowd toward the car. Auntie shifted around to the door at that point, and I could see her eyes bulge as she saw me. Her face had agony written all over it. Oh, my God, I said, Auntie's having a *real* heart attack! She was also trying to open the door or roll down the window now. She seemed to be suffocating and as I reached the car, pushing aside two devotees who were too stunned to retaliate, she collapsed against the seat while the driver, who had gotten back into the car, leaned over her trying unsuccessfully to roll down the window himself. Then I remembered, this was the car that had the door that wouldn't open from the inside. I grabbed the handle, but now it wouldn't open from the outside either. Auntie must have absentmindedly locked it when she got in. Desperation. What should I do? All I could think of were those police movies where when someone needs to get through a window, they smash their fist into it.

171

So that's what I did. Big mistake! Do you know how hard a car window is? I thought for a minute I had broken my hand. It was like the comedy routine where the little guy trying to be Clint Eastwood throws himself against the door to break it down and only ends up pulverizing his shoulder.

My brain did finally start working, however. You remember those big walking shoes I left home with. Well, they wore out in the Alps so I bought a Swiss pair and if you think the others were big and tough looking! In short, I kicked the window in—though I had to give those two poor devotees another shove to make room. They were pretty pissed off by then and when things really began to unravel, I thought they'd murder someone on the spot.

I reached in, unlocked the door and pulled it open. Auntie rolled out and collapsed to the ground like a sack of corn. She obviously needed air, so I yanked at her robes. Unfortunately, as I did so, her hair came down and her beard came off.

A woman nearby screamed and the two p.o.ed devotees whom I had shoved began to jabber at everyone around. Word spread like the proverbial wildfire. Surprise. Panic. A babble of tongues. Hysteria was next, I could tell, and pandemonium after that.

"Go, go" I yelled at the driver. "Get this bleeping rattletrap out of here." I've written "bleeping" just in case some young innocent gets hold of this, but I'm sure you know what it stands for. The man reached for the ignition key, but then Raj, who had watched all the foregoing in a daze, shouted a commanding "NO!" and got out of the car (the back door, unfortunately, worked fine).

Without another word, he pulled the sash from his face, revealing his beard, and started yanking at his clothes and ended by facing the crowd and throwing his arms out wide. Oh Ginny, I wish you'd been there. In pulling at his clothes, he managed to collapse one of his breasts while making the other bulge out more. I'm telling you, Raj standing there wearing a reddish-brown sari and big black beard, with a chest looking like a cross between Twiggy and Dolly Parton, was a sight I'll never forget.

All of which would have been very funny if I hadn't been scared bleepless by what was happening with that crowd. Here was Auntie, looking half-man-half-woman, lying on the ground gasping for breath.

172

And here was their Guruji standing before them like a deranged clown, also looking half-man-half-woman. It wasn't hard for the ones nearby to detect a scam, and soon they all knew and were suddenly really angry. A roar of fury and disillusionment went up. The crowd began to move and surge. And then it happened.

It was weird. The timing was so perfect you'd think it had been planned.

Imagine it, Ginny. Conjure up total pandemonium, sheer anarchy, a mass of people whose adoration is turning to rage. The man who had promised to relieve the drought that was killing the country had turned out to be a fraud. Tense situation, right? Suddenly, the heavens open up and dump on us one of the heaviest bursts of rain I have ever seen, a tropical shower that only lasted for a few minutes but came down in buckets and drenched everything. It reminded me of one of those midafternoon tropical outbursts I saw when I was in Kuala Lumpur when the kids rushed out and danced in the streets.

In Yalakki, the shower stopped as abruptly as it had begun. The hot scorching sun seemed to continue shining without a blip right through the downpour. What kind of meteorological phenomenon caused it I have no idea.

The crowd, of course, was just as astounded as I was. They stopped in their tracks, frozen. The silence was almost scary, like in a movie when the heroine is about to be attacked and they stop playing background music. Obviously, they were in a state of shock, though of course they were also grateful for the rain. They were looking at the sky or at Raj (even in his ridiculous costume) in reverence. It was a mystical experience. God had appeared to them. Their Swamiji, in whatever weird dress, had brought rain as he had promised. It was both a miracle and an omen of better things to come.

Raj, who had folded his arms together in a prayerful gesture, now lifted them upward, his eyes closed, his face etched in a beatific expression.

"Raj," I said in a whisper as I sidled closer to him.

He opened his eyes and I heard him say, as much to himself as to anyone else, "Now I can leave. God has given me permission!" Then he quickly got into the car and nodded vigorously to the driver. The driver bowed to him and took the wheel. The crowd jostled to make way as the car backed and turned and eased out of the crowd, then sped towards Bangalore, raising clouds of dust from the road that was already as dry as it had been before the rain. The crowd started to chant "Guruji, Guruji," and kept bowing in the direction of the speeding car.

Thus Raj departed from Yalakki, not tarred and feathered for being the con artist he is, but as a hero, his reputation not only intact but fixed in the heavens. What an ending! In a movie it'd give *Casablanca* a run for its money.

By the way, Auntie did not die. She was only suffering from a mild heatstroke. The downpour revived her.

As the crowd slowly dispersed, I wandered around trying to get a sense of their reactions. The people seemed happy, though I couldn't say definitely since they weren't speaking much English—until I ran into Sharma, the reporter, again and he confirmed it. Their only regret was that Raj had gone. They hoped he would return. Raj had a future not only in Yalakki, the reporter said, but in all India once the story got around (in which he assured me he would play a part).

Two of the most disappointed people were of course Vimala and her eldest brother. "Cheap magic," Vimala said with as much sarcasm as possible. "It will be investigated," her eldest brother threatened. "I have big connections in police department." I turned to leave, but Vimala, somewhat less than daintily, held me by the shirtsleeve. "So after all this hanky-panky Saroja gives birth only to a daughter," she said scornfully. "My son Kittu will be going to college in the United States when he is old enough. He has already received offer of admission from American business college in Nevada. I will personally carry on antipropaganda in U.S. against Yalakki holy man," she added, letting go of my sleeve.

She was almost sputtering with rage. I did not even bother to quiz her on how Kittu could possibly have been admitted to a college in the U.S.—he's only a kid, for God's sake. Sour grapes with a vengeance.

A couple of days later in Bangalore, where I was unsuccessfully trying to track down Raj, I read about the event in a long feature article in the *Deccan Herald*. Sharma, the reporter, was true to his word. He proclaimed Raj the Guruji of Yalakki. I was going to enclose the clipping with this letter, but I can't seem to find it. I'm sure Raj knows the significance of what happened. He might even think he can work real miracles. In any case, as the reporter said, Raj has a great future here in India if he wants it. Bona fide holy men have it made. Of course, all this wouldn't hurt either if he went back to the U.S. and took over Thelma's Avalon Ashram, though I imagine the possibility of staying here and sticking it to Vimala and her brothers would be very tempting. Well, I guess we'll just have to wait for the next episode.

Love, Jeff

5

Back in Avalon Ginny and Thelma, who had photocopied and were now sharing all of Raj's and Jeff's letters no matter to whom they were addressed, looked at each other over their glasses of wine in the expensive restaurant they had decided to treat themselves to.

Thelma had returned to Avalon to begin work on the Avalon Ashram project.

"So, Raj escaped," Ginny said.

"Yes, and I'm certain he will make it to Madras and get his six-month tourist visa from the American consulate. I've already written a letter and signed an affidavit to vouch for him. Glen Hutchinson's nephew, Todd, is the consul in Madras. I've asked Glen through his wife Ethel to ask Todd to push Raj's visa application through when he shows up there. Ethel was National President of the American Business and Professional Women's Association. We became quite close. I organized a dinner for her when she stepped down. If Raj has escaped Yalakki, it's only a matter of time before he'll be in San Francisco and I'll be there to pick him up," said Thelma with overflowing confidence.

"What happens after the six months?" Ginny asked.

"By then we'll have developed the Avalon Ashram. There'll be the members or devotees or followers . . . whatever they're called. That means Raj is their pastor. So they'll petition immigration to allow him to continue to minister to their spiritual needs. Raj can then become a permanent resident. Oh, I've researched this entire project."

"You're really serious about this Ashram, aren't you?" Ginny said.

"I certainly am."

"But suppose Raj doesn't come? Don't forget, after the Yalakki rain incident he's going to have quite a reputation in India. Being a holy man can be a pretty lucrative profession if you've pulled off a miracle or two."

"But, Ginny, look at all the good he can do. We have our own drought problem, too—a drought of the soul. I think what happened in Yalakki shows that Raj is not a phony. It would be so exciting and worthwhile to help lay the foundations for bringing his spirituality to Americans."

Ginny looked at her friend quizzically. Two things, at least, were sure: Raj had it made whether he remained in India *or* came back to the States, and he and Thelma were equally wacky.